An Environment for Murder

An Environment for Murder

by

ROD DECKER

Signature Books   Salt Lake City
1994

to Chris

Cover design by Ron Stucki
Cover photo illustration by Thomas Anastasion

∞ *An Environment for Murder* was printed on acid-free paper and meets the permanence of paper requirements of the American Standard for Information Sciences. This book was composed, printed, and bound in the United States.

98   97   96   95   94   6   5   4   3   2

Library of Congress Cataloging-in-Publication Data
Decker, Rod
    An environment for murder / Rod Decker.
        p.   cm.
    I. Title.
PS3554.E188E58   1994
813'.54—dc20

                                                    94-3608
                                                    CIP

one

Huge Power Plant Coming to S. Utah; Environment- alist Says It's "Murder"

by Al Cannon

A long and toilsome career in journalism has taught me many things. I can read the inner workings of the establishment, discern hidden designs controlling public events, and use a dozen different tricks to slip into a newsroom when I am late for work.

On this particular morning, I strode through the center of the large newsroom at a businesslike but unhurried pace, as befits my moderate corpulence, graying brown hair, and status as senior reporter. I passed several colleagues already at their desks pursuing the day's news on the phone or typing it into their word processors, but I pretended to be too preoccupied to notice them. As I walked, I took a reporter's notebook from the side pocket of my old-and-faithful tweed jacket and turned through the pages as if trying to find the notes I needed, so

1

I would be ready to start writing when I reached my desk.

To all appearances I might have just concluded an exclusive breakfast interview with an important news source, and arrived at the *Utah Telegram* in time to dash off a story for the first edition. Maybe no one would notice I was tardy and suffering from a hangover.

"Al," city editor Barry Bowen shouted. I had hoped to avoid him this morning. He delights in harassing reporters, especially those who rely on ability rather than drudgery. As I turned and walked towards him, sitting fat and imperious at the head of the city desk, I reviewed several plausible but evasive replies I had prepared in case he asked me where I'd been.

"Here's a story for you," Bowen said, handing me a piece of paper. "I was worried you might not get here in time to cover it." Bowen held the paper out towards me with one hand, but he kept his eyes on his word processor where he was editing stories. He spoke in mild tones, but I detected sarcasm underneath. He suspects I am lazy and deceitful. On another occasion, I would have pointed out how this groundless mistrust detracts from a pleasant work environment. But considering my compromised tactical position this morning, I thought it best to take the paper and walk away.

The paper was a press release: "From the Office of Governor Parley Smith Wells." He would make an important announcement about the California Commonwealth Power Project at the State Capitol. The CalCom story is one I cover. A press conference is always welcome—an easy day's work. I left the newsroom quickly before I fell into bad company.

Utah's Capitol sits on a hill overlooking the city and is constructed of local granite, about the color of my gray tweed jacket. It looks like the national Capitol, but is smaller and more pleasingly proportioned. I parked my beige Chevette in one of several spaces near the front steps marked "Press Only." Getting out of an open jeep, with a worn "Don't Californicate Utah" sticker on its rear bumper, was environmentalist Paul Rambeau wearing a plaid shirt, knit tie, and pressed Levis. His hair and spade-shaped beard are sun-bleached. He has no mustache.

"These spaces are reserved for reporters," I said, and smiled to show I was joking.

"Somebody needs to watch the reporters in this town," Rambeau said. He didn't smile. He rarely does.

He waited for me at the bottom of the broad stone steps, then he trotted up the stairs two at a time and had to wait for me again at the top. When I caught up, I leaned against one of the rough granite columns and lit a cigarette to help me catch my breath.

The view from the Capitol is dominated by the Mormon Church Office Building, a high, white shaft that presides over downtown. It alone rises high enough to stare at the Capitol nose-to-nose. Around its feet, Salt Lake City spreads in perfectly square blocks, symbolic of civic rectitude. The streets are laid true to the compass. State Street, for example, begins at the Capitol and runs straight as the part in a missionary's hair for twenty miles across the valley floor. Today it vanished gradually in a gray haze like the limits of human understanding.

"Look at that gunk," Rambeau said, directing the point of his beard at the haze. "It's ugly."

Actually, the view was rather scenic. The smog lay low in the valley, as in the bottom of a bowl. The granite-topped Wasatch Mountains rose above smog and other human squalor into the clean, blue sky. Foremost among the tall peaks, Mount Olympus turned its craggy face towards the city, as if brooding over events below.

On a lower foothill to the east, appropriate to merely secular knowledge, a large, whitewashed "U" advertised the University of Utah. And across the valley to the west, the mountains opened to the Great Salt Lake, a vague brown patch in the autumn sun, surrounded by miles of bare, brown desert that waits patiently to reclaim the green and ordered city, and reminds us of the vanity of all the works of humankind.

I threw my cigarette butt into a standing ashtray and followed Rambeau into the Capitol. We walked through the rotunda to the board room where the governor holds press conferences. Two dozen people were already waiting. They stood talking in small groups or sat in straight-backed chairs upholstered in beige leather. I recognized state legislators, business leaders, and high-level state and federal bureaucrats. I was happy to see them all. A crowd of important people means the governor will make an important announcement, and that means a better story for me. Besides, they would all be present for quick interviews after the governor was finished, easing the task of a hardworking reporter.

Three TV photographers, young men in Levis and polo shirts, were raising spotlights on spindly poles and placing microphones with colorful station insignia on the podium at the front of the room. Beside the podium was an easel holding flip charts. The cover said, "California Commonwealth, The Utah Project."

The room became quiet as Governor Wells entered from a side door that leads to his private office. The governor is tall and portly with wavy silver hair and a red face. He strode to the podium and paused briefly to look at the crowd, while the television photographers focussed their cameras. Then he assumed the Brigham Position.

Near Salt Lake City's principal crossroads stands an heroic-sized bronze statue of Brigham Young. Our Founder is portrayed with his left arm outstretched, palm upwards, in a gesture of welcome or display. His face is benign; his eyes gaze into the distance, contemplating Utah's future greatness. Governor Wells stands in the posture of that statue on appropriate occasions to remind Utahns that he stands in the political tradition of Brigham Young.

The governor held the pose for several seconds, allowing the cameramen to frame the shot correctly. Then he said, "When our pioneer forefathers came to this land, they vowed to make the desert blossom as the rose."

Rambeau, sitting beside me, groaned, "Every time they say that, they do something ugly."

"Now we have a special opportunity to make that dream even more fulfilled," the governor said, staring sincerely into the Channel 5 camera. "The California Commonwealth Power Company has chosen Utah as the site of the largest, coal-fired electric power generating station in the free world," he proclaimed. "Of course, my administration has worked proactively with CalCom to select the best possible location. And let me say how much I appreciate the cooperation of Coleman Bywater, who is in charge of this project." The governor indicated a man in a pin-striped suit sitting in the front row, who nodded and smiled slightly.

Then the governor turned to the flip charts on the easel by the podium and turned the cover to reveal an outline map of Utah with a star in the southeast quadrant labelled "CalCom" and nearby a dot labelled "Persevere." With a sweeping flourish that ended with his finger pointing to the star, the governor said, "We have decided to put the plant here, near the town of Persevere."

"They can't do that. They'll ruin the parks." Rambeau spoke loudly enough to turn heads, and also the Channel 4 TV camera. The Channel 4 reporter eyed Rambeau speculatively, hoping for a disturbance that would improve her story.

Governor Wells was not disturbed. He raised his chin a centimeter and his voice a decibel and continued with his speech, all the while staring sternly at the Channel 4 reporter in an unspoken demand that she return her attention to the proper subject of the news conference, himself, which presently she did.

The governor flipped another chart to reveal a table of numbers, and for the first time he looked down at notes to cite statistics. Total cost of the project would be $10 billion. The governor also noted how much coal the plant would burn, how much electricity it would generate, and how many Utahns it would employ. All of the numbers were very large.

"Utah needs those jobs," the governor said. "We have the highest birth rate in America, and we need economic development so our young people can find work and stay at home." His eyes twinkled. "Why, just last week, Mrs. Wells and I had our twenty-eighth grandchild, and I said to her, 'Mother, we aren't through yet.'" Members of the governor's staff led the audience in an appreciative chuckle at yet another instance of the folksy, family-oriented humor that makes Parley Smith Wells so formidable in Utah elections.

Rambeau stared glumly at the carpet. "He has no shame."

With his red face moist and shining from the television lights, the governor picked up his speaking pace slightly as he approached his peroration. "We will face opposition from the so-called environmentalists and from the big and bloated federal bureaucracies. But we will overcome those obstacles as our pioneer forefathers overcame the deserts and mountains, and we will secure for our posterity the opportunity to live and prosper in Utah,"

Rambeau sprang to his feet. "There's another side to this, you know. You ought to get the other side." He sidled past me towards the TV cameras even before the governor had turned away from the podium. People stood up to leave, and the room filled with the buzz of talk. Some reporters crowded around the governor. I walked over to Coleman Bywater, the man the governor had introduced as head of the CalCom Project in Utah, and introduced myself.

"Oh, yes, Mr. Cannon, I've read your news articles. They're the best explanations we've had of the project, better than anything in the California papers," Bywater said. Reporters are occasionally complimented by people who hope that if they say nice things to a reporter's face, he'll say nice things about them in the newspaper. But Bywater was good at flattery and I thanked him. Bywater was as tall as the governor, but slender where the governor was stout. He had black-rimmed glasses and spoke like an accountant.

"What do you think of the governor's announcement?"

"It's a good deal all around," Bywater said. "California needs the power. Utah needs the economic growth. I think everyone benefits."

"The governor has sold Utah out. California gets the power. California gets the profits. All Utah gets is the pollution." It was Rambeau, talking loudly to TV cameras.

Bywater looked over to see who was talking, then he replied to what Rambeau was saying, though he spoke quietly to me. "Actually the governor drove a hard bargain for Utah. We'll use Utah coal, and Utah labor, and we'll spend a third of the total construction costs on pollution-control equipment."

I thanked Bywater and hurried to catch Merrill Gott of the BLM before he left the room. The federal government owns more than half of all the land in Utah, and despite anything the governor or Rambeau said, it would be Gott and his bosses in Washington who decided the fate of any big project in the state.

"Could I ask you a couple of questions?" I asked.

"Oh, hi, Al. Sure." Gott turned to a skinny, dark-haired young man beside him. "Al, this is Orson Jones. He's writing the environmental impact statement for the project."

"That must keep you busy," I said as we shook hands.

"Too busy," he said and grinned.

"Maybe I could come talk to you about what you're doing," I said to Jones.

Gott interrupted, "We like to direct press inquiries to our media relations office, Al."

I nodded and asked Gott what he thought of the governor's announcement. Despite what the governor had said about the federal bureaucracy, Gott was not big and bloated. He was short and wiry. A ginger mustache sprouted from his wrinkled face.

"We've been monitoring the state process," he said. "Of course we couldn't make any decisions on permits until after we've completed the environmental impact assessment process." He nodded at Jones.

"How does it look so far?" I asked.

"We wouldn't want to speculate," Gott said. Federal bureaucrats hardly ever want to speculate.

A less experienced journalist would have felt obliged to interview Rambeau. But Rambeau was still talking on television, and I needed to get back to the *Telegram* soon to make the noon deadline for today's paper. So while I still remembered, I wrote down what Rambeau had said about the governor selling out Utah and about the plant ruining the parks. On my way out, I heard Rambeau talking to Channel 2.

"The parks need big vistas," Rambeau said, holding his hands wide apart. "This would just murder the big vistas. It would irreparably reduce the scenic value of the parks."

As soon as I finished writing, I slipped out of the newsroom for a leisurely lunch at Lamb's Cafe. Then I returned to my apartment, turned off the phone, mixed a bourbon and water, fell onto my couch to read Macaulay's essay on Clive. With a mind satisfied by a daily task attacked with vigor and completed with dispatch, I slipped into an afternoon nap. Barry Bowen had run the story on A-1. In all, a day of journalistic achievement gracefully accomplished. Exactly the kind of day a senior reporter always strives for but too seldom gets.

two

Bradford Hastings, publisher of the *Utah Telegram,* is a small, tidy man who works in a large, tidy office. "Thanks for coming, Al," he said, as I entered in response to a summons from his secretary. He smiled to show he is a friendly boss, folded the *Wall Street Journal* he had been reading into its original shape, and laid it neatly on the corner of his large, bare desk.

Hastings always wears a no-iron white shirt, and unlike every other man who works at the *Telegram*, he never loosens his tie. Past front pages of the *Telegram,* framed in glass, hang on his office walls: "Germany Surrenders, War Ends in Europe," "It's Ike by a Landslide," "A Man Walks on the Moon," "Reagan Reelected, Wins 49 States." Hastings mounts moments that encourage and inspire him.

Hastings began his career as a reporter two or three years after I did. We had different styles. His desk was always the cleanest in the newsroom, mine the messiest. He arrived early, I came late. He aspired to help community leaders clarify their positions and secure popular consent; I sought to expose, tease, and confound them. He had risen through a series of editorial positions to his present eminence. I was still a reporter.

"Al, we just wanted to tell you the governor called and said your piece yesterday on his announcement was first rate. We want to add our compliments to his. It was a real *Telegram* job." He smiled again.

I said "thank you," but was wondering what Hastings wanted. He compliments his workers because praise is cheaper than higher wages. But he doesn't call us into his office especially to say nice things without an ulterior motive.

"We suppose you've heard about the governor's dinner for the CalCom Project next Friday," Hastings said.

"No, I haven't."

Hastings put his elbows on the arms of his high-backed, black-leather, swivel chair and steepled his fingers in front of his chest. Though he didn't mean to show it, I could tell he was pleased. He's always pleased when he finds out something before one of his reporters. It shows once again that he could still succeed as a working newsman if his management talents had not called him to a higher assignment.

"He's inviting the top leaders of the state," Hastings explained. "He wants us all to get together and form a united front to show the federal people that we mean business on this CalCom Project."

"I see," I said, though in fact I still didn't see why Hastings had called me to his office.

"The governor wants some of the leaders from business and the community to respond. He asked us to speak on behalf of the news media." I was beginning to see what Hastings wanted. "Al, this shows that top people recognize the good work we're doing here at the *Telegram*. It's a real compliment to you, too." I nodded. "Al, we looked at our calendar, and we're just swamped. We were wondering if you could outline a few issues for us." Hastings smiled.

"When do you need it?"

"We realize you're busy, too, Al, and we wouldn't ask you, but this is an opportunity to do a lot of good for the *Telegram*. It shows we're a leader in our field."

"When do you need it?"

"This has to be a *Telegram* team effort, Al, and you're our senior man on this story."

"When do I need to have it done?"

"If you could get it to us in a couple of days, say Thursday morning, we'd have time to go over it."

"How long should it be?"

"I think we should start with some jokes, you know, topical stuff about environmentalists and things like that. Then we need some good analysis, you know, show them how we go into depth here at the *Telegram*. And we want an enthusiastic ending, show them the *Telegram* is on the Utah team." Hastings made a fist and punched the air as he said "Utah team."

"How long does it need to be?"

"The governor said five minutes."

"I'll need some time to work on it."

Hastings nodded. "We'll tell Barry you're on special assignment."

"Okay." I got up to leave.

"Oh, and Al," Hastings paused, choosing his words. "This is important for the *Telegram*, so don't get . . . don't get sidetracked."

"Okay," I said, and left.

three

Coal Ruling Could Kill CalCom Plan

by Al Cannon

I sat at my desk thinking about Hastings's speech. I could write it in half-a-day, but I could stretch the special assignment out over the rest of the week. Once again, it seemed, a modest talent with words released me from the drudgery of daily news and brought me some well deserved time to loaf.

My phone rang. It was Paul Rambeau. "I've got something you might want to know," he said. "I've already given it to the *Los Angeles Times*, and they're definitely interested, but it needs local coverage, too."

"What?"

"The Bureau of Land Management just sent CalCom a letter saying they can't have the coal on public land. So now they've got the world's biggest coal-fired plant, and they don't have any coal." Rambeau suppressed a chortle. Over the phone it sounded like a snort.

"Have you seen the letter?"

"No, but I have a very reliable source."

"Who?"

"I can't reveal the name, but it was a very knowledgeable person."

"Was it Orson Jones?"

"How . . . Why do you say that?" Rambeau was unable to keep the surprise from his voice.

"Well, he's a very knowledgeable source, and yesterday at the governor's announcement, I asked to interview him, and his boss didn't want me to. I thought maybe he and his boss disagreed about something, and so maybe he is leaking information."

"Yes, well, I can neither confirm nor deny the name of the source," Rambeau said. "Of course the establishment has mobilized. You can't believe the pressure CalCom is putting on the BLM to get the letter withdrawn. That's why we need some publicity on it."

"Why hasn't there been anything said publicly so far?"

"Because CalCom wants it kept quiet so they can get the decision reversed quickly, and no one will know the difference." Rambeau spoke slowly as if explaining something obvious to someone who wasn't very smart.

I thanked him and we hung up. I considered what to do. I could go to Barry Bowen and remind him I was on special. He would give the story to another reporter. But it sounded like a good story. In a long and checkered career, I have done many foolish things, but I have never given a good story to another reporter.

In the phone book under United States Government, Department of Interior, Bureau of Land Management, there was a half column of numbers. I dialed the one at the bottom, "For Numbers Not Listed Above." After talking to a receptionist and then a secretary, I got through to Orson Jones. "I've been told to refer all media inquiries to our media affairs office," he said.

"I heard the Bureau sent a letter to CalCom saying they can't have the coal they need. Do you know about that?" I asked.

Jones hesitated, "I'd like to talk to you, Mr. Cannon, but I could get into real trouble if my name got in the paper or anything."

"I won't put your name in the paper. I promise I won't even say we talked," I said.

"Why don't you call public affairs. I can give you Jack Hampton's phone number, I have it right here."

"Mr. Jones, I heard the Bureau is keeping the letter quiet, and CalCom is applying pressure to get the Bureau to withdraw it. If that's true, I don't think public affairs will be helpful."

Jones paused again. "It sounds like you've got some pretty good sources on this already. I don't think you need me."

"I don't know enough to write a story, and if you won't help me, I don't know where I'll go. This power plant is supposed to be a public decision, and I don't see why the public shouldn't be told the facts."

There was another moment of silence while Jones thought. "Maybe we could just meet for a soda, or something," Jones said. "It wouldn't be official. We could just talk."

"Could you meet me at Siegfried's in fifteen minutes?" I asked.

"I think that would be okay. You won't put my name in the paper?"

"I promise I won't use your name." We rang off.

At Siegfried's, a stocky, sixtyish woman was laying links of bratwurst by the grill in preparation for lunch. The place smelled of fat and spices. I poured myself a cup of coffee, took a table in the back, and lit a cigarette. I was just taking the first careful sip of hot coffee when Jones came through the glass front door. I waved, and he tossed his head in recognition. He had a sinewy walk, learned from long hikes over mountains and deserts. He wore poplin pants and a long-sleeved, light-blue dress shirt with the sleeves rolled halfway up his forearms.

Utah may be the only place where men glance at each other's chests when they meet for the first time. The outline of the religious underwear worn by Mormons shows through a man's shirt. So I guessed Jones was a devout Mormon even before he poured himself a Seven-Up at 10:30 in the morning. I snuffed out my cigarette, half-smoked.

"I've never done anything like this before," he said, as he sat down. "I kind of feel like a traitor or something, sneaking off like this." He looked around the room furtively, as if he were afraid of seeing someone he knew.

This was not a promising beginning. Sources who feel like traitors are unlikely to divulge prizewinning information to an inquiring reporter. I tried to reassure him. "It's public business, and I think the public has a right to know what's going on," I said, taking the moral high ground.

"You're right there," he said. "I sort of think of this as helping the Bureau to do its job."

That was much better. I decided I'd start asking questions while he still thought we were being helpful. "Has the Bureau told the CalCom people they can't have the coal they need?"

"Not exactly," Jones said. "The letter I sent said the leases were questionable. We have to look at them. We still haven't made a final decision."

"The letter *you* sent?" Jones might have been approaching thirty, but he still looked like a fresh-faced college sophomore. I was surprised that someone so junior was holding up a $10-billion project, and the governor's dream of blossoming desert.

He heard the surprise in my voice, and looked straight at me raising his chin in defense of youthful dignity. "Yes, as head of the environmental impact assessment team, I thought I should tell

CalCom as soon as I saw a problem. As a courtesy." His eyes were very blue, and his nose was dusted with freckles.

I nodded. His point was taken. He took a victorious sip of Seven-Up through his straw.

"Why is the government saying CalCom might not get the coal?"

"The government owns the coal. It's under government land. Before CalCom can mine it, they need to get a lease from the federal government, and they have to pay fees and royalties." Jones spoke in neutral tones, as young bureaucrats are trained to do, letting the facts speak for themselves.

"I didn't even know there was coal in that area," I said.

"It's never been developed." Jones furrowed his dark eyebrows. "The coal is under this plateau, hundreds of square miles. It sticks out around the edges. You can see seams of coal from Persevere. So people have known it was there, and they've been staking claims ever since the country was settled. A few of them even tried to open mines, but they couldn't make it go. They left this mess of overlapping claims and mineral disputes." When he thought of untidy land administration, Jones wrinkled his nose as if a fly had landed in his Seven-Up. "Then a speculator came along and bought up the old claims, filed new ones, put together a big package and sold it to CalCom."

"Do you know his name?" I asked.

"Yeah, Vassos. Nick Vassos. He's a colorful old guy, lives in Price. I guess he's spent most of his life trying to put a big coal deal together."

"Sounds like he succeeded this time."

"Yeah."

"So why aren't the leases valid?"

"The rules are changing. We used to just promote development on the public lands. Keep things orderly, encourage people to use the resources. But anymore we're supposed to be more aggressive managers, get the best return for the public, protect the environment, things like that. Soon we're going to invalidate all the old coal leases and have a new auction for coal rights on every parcel. So this project's kind of caught between the old and new rules."

"Didn't CalCom know the rules were changing?"

"Yes, they got a letter from the Bureau that we would honor their leases if the project proved appropriate in all other respects."

"So your letter . . ."

"Yes, my letter took a slightly tougher line. I think whoever wrote the first letter didn't realize how sloppy and fouled-up those old leases were." Jones allowed himself a wry smile. "It used to be a joke when I was growing up in Persevere how fast-talking outsiders would come to town and try to get rich off coal claims."

"You grew up in Persevere?"

"Yeah, I'd still live there if I could figure out a way to make a living."

"Do you object to what the plant will do to the area?" I was thinking that people who risk their jobs to leak information to reporters usually have reasons. If Jones was angry about the plant ruining his home town, that might be his reason.

He shrugged. "It's not my favorite thing. My personal feelings don't really matter much." Then he leaned forward across the table. "What does matter is that this is the biggest project we've ever had here and we ought to do it right. If we go through the process fairly and make an honest decision, and it turns out I'm wrong about the coal, that's okay. It won't bother me, not even with all it's cost me. But we shouldn't make a hasty political decision just because of pressure from some big California corporation." Jones was no longer the neutral civil servant.

"Has CalCom put pressure on the Bureau?"

"You bet they . . ." He stopped and frowned, making sure he spoke accurately. "Well, I'm assuming the governor was speaking for them when he came to our office."

"That's unusual isn't it, for the governor to come to your office?"

"First time it's ever happened so far as I know. We always go up to the Capitol."

"What did he say?"

"I don't know. I wasn't invited to the meeting."

"How do you know it was about CalCom?"

"Gott said it was when he talked to me after the meeting. I think the governor was upset. I know Gott was angry."

"What did he say to you?"

"He said I'd exceeded my authority. He relieved me as head of the environmental impact assessment team."

"That's hard," I said. "Does it hurt your career?"

Jones nodded. "I'll have to leave the Bureau. You don't get promoted after you've been relieved like that."

"You're still there now."

"Yeah, I've got a year or so before I have to leave. Know anyone who wants to hire an out-of-work land manager?" Jones shrugged. "I did what I thought was right. I mean the professionals I work with say they admire what I did. They just don't say it publicly." He sipped on his straw, and the Seven-Up in the bottom of his glass made a discouraged gurgle. "I don't let it get me down. I don't have so much to do at the office, so I just go jogging more. I've got this run goes up by the U Mountain, that's a—"

"I've got to get going or I won't make today's paper," I said. When he talked of jogging, Jones wiggled like a young puppy. But like an old dog, I dislike even the thought of exercise.

We shook hands and left. I walked up West Temple back to the *Telegram*. Between the tall, boxy, downtown office buildings I could see the U Mountain where Jones jogged. I had a problem. I couldn't quote Jones by name. But I didn't want to base the entire story on one unnamed source, and I didn't know where I could get the story confirmed. When I got back to the newsroom I told Bowen, "I've got a good one. The CalCom Project may be dead."

"I'll see if they want it on A-1," he said.

Then I hurried to my desk, called the governor's office, and asked for press secretary Janet Lundmon. "I heard the governor is fighting with the BLM over CalCom's coal rights," I said.

"Where did you hear that, Al?"

"So it's true then?"

"Wait a minute. I didn't say that."

"I heard the BLM sent CalCom a letter saying they might not get permission to mine the coal, and the governor went to the BLM office to try to get the letter withdrawn."

"I don't know about this, Al."

"What have you heard?"

"I'll have to talk to the governor and get back to you."

"Hurry, please, I'm on a noon deadline." I didn't think she'd get back in time, so I called public affairs at the Bureau of Land Management and asked for Jack Hampton. He said he didn't know anything about it, but he'd check and call me back, maybe this afternoon or tomorrow.

That left CalCom, and if they were working to keep the letter quiet they wouldn't be likely to tell me about it. But I had to give them a chance to comment. I called the Salt Lake office, and the secretary put me through to Coleman Bywater.

"I heard the BLM sent you a letter saying you may not be able to mine the coal you need," I said.

"Yes, it's true, federal officials have questioned the validity of our coal leases," Bywater said matter-of-factly. "We'd rather it had not become public at this time."

I was surprised by his candor. "Is that a problem for the project?"

"It certainly could be. We can't go ahead without a firm supply of coal, of course. But putting these projects together is largely a matter of solving one problem after another, and we're hopeful we can resolve this one."

"How?"

"We believe the BLM ruling is wrong. We're asking them to change it. We believe—"

I interrupted, "I hear you've been pressuring the Bureau to withdraw the letter."

"Mr. Cannon, if you know of any way to pressure a federal agency, I wish you'd tell me."

"I heard you had the governor talk to them."

"You'll have to ask the governor what he's doing. All I can say is that I'm sure he's working for the interests of the people of Utah."

"Are you going to court?"

"I hope not. To be honest, the letter was well drafted. It will be hard to argue legally against the Bureau's discretion. And even if we won, it would take so long the project might be dead, anyway."

"So what can you do?"

"We're looking to acquire another lease that could meet the plant's needs."

"Where?"

"Well, we're already at a disadvantage in those negotiations, as you can understand, and I really don't want to release any more details now."

I thanked Bywater and hung up. I had to get writing to make the noon deadline. After I'd written the first three paragraphs, Bradford Hastings's secretary, Edith, called to me across the newsroom. "Al, the governor wants to talk to you. He's on Mr. Hastings's line."

"Put him on my line," I said. I kept typing as I talked to the governor.

"Janet tells me you've got some story about trouble with CalCom's coal. Believe me, Al, that's a big mistake. I'm just calling to tell you that the BLM didn't send any letter to CalCom. This is really not a story."

"Coleman Bywater said CalCom received the letter," I said.

"Coleman said that?" The governor's voice rose in surprise. "I don't know why he'd say that. It can only make things worse."

"I heard you went to the BLM office and asked them to withdraw the letter."

"You bet I did, and I'll go again, too. We're going to get this thing straightened out," the governor said.

I typed the governor's words directly into the story:

```
Governor Parley Smith Wells went person-
ally to the BLM office to ask for the with-
drawal of the letter. "I'll go again, too,"
the governor said. "We're going to get this
straightened out."
```

"Al, I'm asking you to hold off on this story."

"I'm sorry, governor, I'm writing it for today's paper."

"If Bradford Hastings were there, I know he'd wait. Brad's always cooperative."

"Well, you could talk to Barry Bowen. He's in charge when Hastings isn't here."

I transferred the governor over to Bowen while I finished the story. Then I went to stand at Bowen's elbow while he edited the story on his word processor.

"They'll take it on A-1," he said, without looking up from the screen. He had turned the governor's request down, too.

Completing a good story on deadline exhilarates a reporter, especially a story that irritates the governor. But I kept remembering Orson Jones and how his bureaucratic mask failed to hide his hurt. He did what he thought was right, but now he was excluded from a project he cared about, an outcast in his office with a blighted career.

four

Wednesday morning I strode into the newsroom late and unafraid. I had a good story in yesterday's paper, and I could fend off bosses and chores with my special assignment for the publisher.

"Big story, Al-babes," Mary Beth Kearney said as I passed her desk. She is a red-headed reporter, who says she wants to become a "respected professional journalist" but is too young to know the contradiction.

But I barely had time to bask in her praise when I found that not everyone shared her high opinion of the story. Bradford Hastings's secretary, Edith, had been waiting for my arrival, and she hallooed across the newsroom. "Al, Al, Mr. Hastings wants to see you in his office."

Barry Bowen was already sitting in Hastings's office. As I entered, he looked at his watch. Hastings had turned his profile to Bowen and was looking at "Clinton Beats Bush," a headline mounted on his wall that he stares at in dark and bitter moods. Hastings swiveled, sat up straight when he saw me, and smiled to show he is a civil boss and we are all on the same team here at the *Telegram,* but he quickly became grave as I sat down.

"We were just saying, Al, we received a disturbing call from Governor Wells this morning about that story you wrote yesterday."

"Yes, I talked to him as I was writing it. He seemed to think we shouldn't run the story."

"The governor said he told you the story was inaccurate, but you ran it in the *Telegram* anyway," Hastings said.

"Did he tell you any specific inaccuracies? I'm not aware of any."

"The governor told us . . ." Hastings looked down for notes on his desk, and paused to find his place. "The governor said he told you that the BLM didn't send a letter to CalCom, and you went right ahead with the story saying they did."

"The story was correct. Coleman Bywater confirmed that Cal-Com received the letter," I said.

Hastings looked pained. "We noticed you quoted Coleman. The governor says he can't understand why Coleman would say those things. They can only hurt the project."

"Maybe he believes in telling the truth," I said.

Hastings leaned forward over his desk and asked in his most prosecutorial tone, "Did Coleman come to you with the information?"

"No, I got it somewhere else and called Bywater for confirmation."

"Who gave you the information?"

"I promised I wouldn't tell."

"There, you see." Hastings rocked back in his swivel chair as if propelled by the force of his riposte. "Governor Wells personally assured us the letter did not come officially from the Bureau of Land Management. Now here at the *Telegram*, we would rather believe the governor of the state of Utah than some anonymous source, probably an environmentalist."

"Well, the story didn't say the letter came officially from the Bureau of Land Management. There was a letter, and Bywater says they may have to hold up the project to get the problem settled," I said.

"That's just the point," Hastings said, bringing his forefinger down on his desk top. "This story could wreck the project. It's done serious harm, Al."

"No. The BLM people might have done harm when they said CalCom's leases aren't valid, but the story didn't do anything but report the facts," I said.

"That's where you're wrong. The governor told us—now this is off the record." Hastings looked sharply at Bowen and me to make sure we understood he was speaking in confidence. "The governor told us the letter is just a foolish mistake. He said the top man at the Bureau of Land Management . . ." Hastings paused and looked through the notes on his legal pad.

"Gott," I said. "Merrill Gott."

"A Mr. Goat," Hastings said staring at his notes. "The governor said this Mr. Goat, promised to withdraw the letter and let the project go ahead. But now, of course, with all the publicity, he can't just withdraw the letter. The whole thing has to be referred to Washington. The Sierra Clubbers and Friends of the World will be lobbying those bureaucrats, and God knows when they'll ever make a decision."

"I didn't know the governor had a deal," I admitted.

"He had a deal all worked out, and that story ruined it, and it has done serious harm to the project." Now that the inner secrets had been revealed, Hastings expected I would become contrite.

But I wasn't contrite. "First, the governor says the BLM didn't send a letter. Now he's telling you in secret that they did send a letter, and he had a secret deal to get the letter withdrawn. He'd better make up his mind," I said.

Bowen jumped in. "I don't see why we should be protecting some secret deal, anyway. This is public business. They ought not to be doing secret deals."

Hastings opened his mouth and shut it. He decided to abandon argument and rely on authority. "Let's make one thing clear, here. The publisher of the *Telegram* is to be included in policy decisions. Damaging Utah's biggest economic development opportunity in history is a policy decision. Our policy at the *Telegram* is to be on the Utah team, not against it." Hastings's fist punched the air as he said "Utah team."

Then he turned up his palm and lowered his voice to show his subordinates he could be reasonable as well as firm. "All the governor wanted was a chance to explain the facts to the proper decisionmaker. We think he should have had that courtesy."

"You were playing golf," I said.

"We did have some *Telegram* matters to discuss outside the building," Hastings conceded with dignity. "The story could have waited for a day."

Bowen shook his head. "Wait a day and we end up reading it in the *Deseret News*," he said. "This was a good story and we were out front on it. Al, here, did a good job." Bowen was trying to speak calmly, but frustration was showing through his tone.

"Of course we want to be first with the news at the *Telegram*. We stand for aggressive reporting here, and we back our staff all the way in reporting the news," Hastings said. He raised his chin and adopted a bulldog-like expression to show his journalistic courage. "But at the same time, we're not irresponsible." Hastings held up his hand. "We've argued enough. From now on, we want to see any story that might hurt this project before it goes into the *Telegram*. Is that clear?"

"Yeah," Bowen said in a tone that made clear he didn't like it. I nodded.

"It's not that we don't trust you, Barry, or you either, Al. You're two key members of the *Telegram* team." Hastings paused and smiled at us.

"How's that speech coming, Al?" he asked in hearty tones, moving on to pleasanter subjects.

"It'll be ready."

"Good. We really appreciate you helping us out on that. Well, if we're agreed, we can adjourn." Hastings smiled again in approval of a successful meeting.

Bowen and I left Hastings's office together. Bowen shook his head in disgust. "That's a good story you did. That's the kind of story newspapers are supposed to do, and Hastings puts us on a leash. He doesn't want good journalism here. He just wants to suck up to his Chamber-of-Commerce friends."

I shrugged. "We were lucky this time. Hastings was away when the story broke, and we got it in the paper. This one turned out pretty well, as far as these things go."

Bowen turned his head and looked at me sharply. "You don't care. You don't care that you do a good story, and Hastings puts you on a leash?"

"It's always been like that here," I said.

"And you don't care anymore?"

"Barry, I used to think about leaving, or about a story that would break the leash. Something so good that Hastings and his friends would hate it but it would be too big and too good for them to stop it." I turned to walk back to the newsroom. "I haven't thought about it for a while. It won't happen."

Bowen took a couple of quick steps to keep up with me. "Did you see the *Tribune* this morning? They followed us on the story. They hate that. TV stations ran the story last night at 10 and even gave us credit for it. 'The *Utah Telegram* reports,' they said. You'd think when we've scooped the town and everyone else is following us, he'd be pleased, at least for a little while."

"He has to give a speech supporting the project Friday, and he feels like he's got to be especially supportive right now," I said.

Bowen turned to face me again, "Yeah, you're writing that for him, aren't you? That's what that special stuff is all about."

"Yeah."

"You know at an honest paper a reporter wouldn't write a speech in favor of a project and cover it at the same time. At an honest paper they'd say that was unethical."

"Yeah, I know."

"But you don't care."

I shrugged. "Writing a speech is a nice break from writing stories, and I may even get some extra time off."

Bowen looked out over the newsroom. "You know I want to leave, too, but I don't know where I'd go. You could have left. You had offers."

"I don't have any offers now," I said.

five

Mayor Pleads for CalCom

by Al Cannon

I sat at my word processor trying to make up jokes. I've written enough speeches for publishers and other semi-literates to know jokes are the most important part. Hastings would have time for three or four jokes. Then he could orate for three or four minutes. No one would remember anything he said. But if his jokes were funny, people would remember laughing at them. Then afterwards they would tell him he was witty and profound. That would put me in his favor for a week or so.

I thought of some old jokes that would fit. (How many Utahns does it take to change a lightbulb? Four, one to change the bulb and three to fill out the environmental impact statement.) I could put those in. But it would help if I could make up some new ones, too. After thinking for a while, I decided to write the serious part first, the part about making the desert blossom as the rose. My phone rang.

"Are you the feller who wrote about the BLMers taking the coal away from the CalCom project?"

"Yes."

"This is Mayor LaVar Hafen from Persevere. Your story has me so mad I could just cuss."

"Oh?"

"Now, I'm not blaming you. I know you didn't do it. But it seems like anymore the media just reports what the environmentalists and the bureaucrats say. They never tell our side."

"I'd be happy to tell your side, mayor."

"Well, I don't think I can explain very well on the phone. You'd have to come down Persevere and see for yourself."

"I couldn't come today. Are you in Persevere now?"

"No, I'm up Salt Lake. I could come to your office and explain some things."

I didn't want to have to think about Hastings's jokes anymore, so I told the mayor how to get to the *Telegram*. He said he would come right over. I went for a cup of coffee. No use trying to write the speech while waiting for an interview.

When I came back, Mayor Hafen was waiting. He stood just inside the newsroom, clutching his western-style straw hat with both hands. There was a tan line across the middle of his forehead. Above his white forehead, his graying dark hair rolled back in oiled waves. He gave me a strong and calloused handshake, and I guided him across the newsroom to my desk.

"Let me ask you right off, was it really Orson Jones wrote that letter?" he said.

"That's what I was told."

"That hurts us. It's bad enough to have the BLMers try to stop the project, but it really hurts when it's one of your own people."

Hafen shook his head sadly. "You know Orson grew up down in Persevere."

"Do you know him?"

"He's practically family. He's the same age as my boy Tracy, and they sort of grew up together. He was a well respected boy, too, smart, ambitious, and he stuck to business. Of course we were concerned when he joined the BLM. But I never thought he'd do something like this."

"He's just doing his job, isn't he?"

Hafen's jaw tightened, then he nodded in a visible effort to be fair-minded. "Yes, yes, I guess he is. I shouldn't be too hard on him. In fact, I'm going to see him later this afternoon. One of the reasons I wanted to talk to you now is so's I'd have the facts when I meet with Orson later."

"Do most people in Persevere want the power plant as much as you do?"

"I think all of them do. Well, no, that's not quite right. Merle Tanner's boy kind of acts like a hippie. Says he doesn't want the plant, but I think he's just getting attention."

"The project would bring a lot of newcomers. Your town would change, wouldn't it?"

"Yes, I suppose it would. But we got to have something to survive. We been losing our young people since before the Depression. We don't get something soon, our town'll just die."

"You've survived so far without a power plant."

"Yes, a hundred and twenty-six years last April. Founded under the direction of Brigham Young. Course he didn't come hisself. He sent some of the brethren."

"So if you've made it that long, why do you need a power plant now?"

Hafen smiled, his mouth glinting with gold fillings. "You Salt Lakers have it easy up here. You don't know what it's like try to get by in Persevere. The Indians couldn't hardly make it before the

pioneers came. The brethren nearly starved the first winter. They
wrote back to President Young and said they couldn't make it. Have
to move back up to Salt Lake. Brother Brigham wrote back and said
'persevere.' So that's what they named the town."

"Great history."

"My great-grandfather helped settle the town. It's kind of been
family lore."

"You must be proud," I said politely.

"It's not a whole lot to be proud of. Almost everybody in town
has an original settler back somewhere. I guess all it shows is your
line didn't have sense enough to get out." The mayor grinned again.

Then he grew serious and put his hand on my forearm. The nail
on the middle finger was bruised dark purple. "If we don't get this
power plant, we'll be gone in a generation. All we got anymore is
folks my age or older and kids, seems like. And the kids move off
to Salt Lake or California or somewhere as soon as they're old
enough to leave home."

"That's their choice, isn't it?"

"Sure. Sure it's their choice if they want to move." He took his
hand off my arm. "Only now they don't have a choice, not really.
Take my family. I have six. The three oldest have moved away. Two
are starting their own families now. They say they want to come
back home. Only there's no way for them to make a living. I farm
a little, keep store, and bring in a little off being mayor. But for
young people just starting out there's just no way hardly."

The mayor leaned back in his chair and lifted his right ankle
onto his left knee, exposing a brown cowboy boot with round toes
and low heels, comfortable for walking. "We don't have much
down there. But we got coal. We got coal sticking out all over the
country. If we could mine the coal and do something with it, why
then our kids could stay in Persevere and have jobs just as good as
if they moved away. We'd survive."

"Wouldn't it destroy the scenery, pollute the national parks?"

"I don't think so. They put all kinds of equipment on those plants now, keep them from polluting. But you ask people down home if they had to choose, they'd choose the project over the parks. Capitol Reef, Arches, Canyonlands don't bring in much money. Not really. We can't eat the scenery."

"You have the tourist industry, don't you?"

"We get a couple hundred backpackers. They come to town with a pair of cutoffs and a twenty-dollar bill, and they never change either one." He grinned at his local joke. "It's hard to explain. You need to come down to Persevere and see for yourself," he said.

"I'd like to do that, mayor."

"Best time's on Wednesdays. We have our Chamber of Commerce lunch, and a lot of the fellers turn out. You can make it in time for lunch if you leave Salt Lake about seven. Then after lunch I'd be happy to take you out on the project."

"I'll try to come some Wednesday," I said, to be polite.

I would write a story about what the mayor said. That would please Bradford Hastings. But I didn't plan to drive 250 miles to talk to Hafen again.

six

By the time I'd finished writing the story, it was close enough to noon so I could take off to D.B. Cooper's for lunch.

Nick the bartender said, "Hi, Al," and set my usual whiskey and water on the bar without being asked. I hadn't intended to drink at lunch. Hastings wanted his speech tomorrow morning, and while I could certainly write it after several whiskeys I would write faster and better without them. One wouldn't hurt.

I ordered lunch at the bar and made small talk with Nick during the few quiet minutes before the noon rush. Nick brought another whiskey without being asked before I had finished the first. He didn't want me to have to wait after he got busy. I ordered another drink with the shrimp casserole over rice, and I had another with a cigarette after the meal, as I sat and considered.

I could go back to the *Telegram* and write the speech now. In fact, I was getting some good ideas. But when I thought about it, Hastings wouldn't even look at the speech until late tomorrow morning. He said he wanted the speech earlier, but I know Hastings. He pads deadlines expecting you to be late.

I could point to several good news stories I had written during the time I was supposed to be free to work on the speech. Certainly they excused a little tardiness. After all, I had agreed to write the speech as part of an implicit deal that would leave me time to loaf. But I hadn't had any loafing time so far. Of course, Bowen wouldn't give me any time after the speech was done. Fat chance of that.

All things considered, the best course would be to spend the afternoon in D.B.'s, start early in the morning, and have the speech to Hastings by mid-morning or so. That would be fair to me, and besides I'd probably do a better job in the morning when I was fresh.

I might even compose a few jokes right here in D.B.'s. The mingled voices of the lunch crowd, the combined smells of cigarettes, laundered table linen, and polished wood tinged with stale beer made a far more congenial working atmosphere than the *Telegram* newsroom.

I waved at Nick to ask him for a pad of paper on which to jot down a few one-liners. He was busy, but gave me another drink in passing. Then an arm was laid on my shoulders, and a deep, theatrical voice said, "What's news, Al?" It was Jerry Hammond, an attorney who keeps drunk drivers out of jail and cultivates prospective customers in bars when he is not in court. We repaired to a table where he told stories of high drama in Utah's lower courts.

I left D.B.'s at eight, when a two-man band began playing amplified guitars and the place got too noisy. Outside it was raining. You could tell the storm had come across the lake: the wind smelled of salt. I walked to my apartment in the mouth of City Creek Canyon. As I walked past the Mormon temple, I looked up at the granite spires illumined by spotlights. Raindrops made silver darts through the beams of light. On the topmost spire the golden statue of Angel Moroni blew his long horn. The brackish rain splattered on my glasses and fell coldly on my upturned face.

seven

"I Had to Leave Him," Widow Sobs

by Al Cannon

Procrastination has advantages. On Wednesday I had struggled to invent new jokes for Hastings's speech. Thursday morning, on deadline, I knew there was no time for originality. I put in the old jokes. After the jokes, the rest was easy. I was finishing up by nine when Bowen yelled across the newsroom, "Cannon, pick up line two."

"I'm on special," I yelled back. Bowen would wring all the work out of me he could. But I hadn't gotten up early this morning to spend an extra long day on Bowen's news stories. My firm intention was to avoid news stories while the speech remained unfinished and to slip out quietly as soon as I delivered it to Hastings.

"Pick up line two and see if you can help us, please," Bowen yelled in a peremptory tone.

I picked up the phone. "This is Cannon," I said.

"Al-babes, this is Mary Beth. I'm at the cop shop. They've got a shooting."

Bowen had stayed on his line. He said, "I think you knew the guy, Al."

"His name was Orson Jones," Kearney said.

"Orson Jones? How bad?"

"He's dead. Someone blew him away up by U Mountain," she said. "You knew him?"

"Yeah, a little." In my mind, I saw the freckles that dusted Orson Jones's nose and his blue eyes.

"Cops say he was shot between six and seven this morning. He went jogging, and he didn't come home. His wife went looking for him. She found the body. Didn't he work for the Forest Service or something?"

"The Bureau of Land Management. He used to be in charge of writing the environmental impact statement for the CalCom Project."

Bowen broke in again. "Kearney, you do the story. Cannon, do a sidebar on who this Jones guy was, and how this will affect the CalCom Project." He hung up before I could argue.

"Do they know who did it?" I asked Kearney.

"No idea. They haven't got a police report out yet, so I don't know everything they have. I talked to Lieutenant Benton. Do you know him?"

"Yes."

"He said they'll give me a copy of the report as soon as he gets it. All they know now is the guy used a shotgun." I said goodbye to Kearney and walked over to Bowen's desk. He was reading stories on his word processor.

"I can't do this this morning," I said.

"You're the only reporter I've got who knows about Jones and this CalCom business. We really need your help."

"I'm on special. We can go talk to Hastings and see which he considers more important."

Bowen turned to look at me. "Hastings doesn't need his speech until tomorrow night. You do this story this morning, and I'll tell him you were late because I pulled you off for this story." Bowen's offer had attractions. I was already late, and his excuse would cover for me as well as give me extra time to write his story. "It's a good story," Bowen added.

I nodded, walked back to my desk, and started looking in the phone book. Orson Jones was listed, but the line was busy. That was to be expected. After sudden tragedy people often call relatives or leave their phones off the hook to avoid reporters and other intruders. Jones's address was listed. He lived in the Avenues, maybe ten minutes from the *Telegram*.

I walked back to Bowen's desk. "I'm going to Jones's house," I said. "I should take a photog."

"Murkett's back there." Murkett was sitting on a tall stool in the photographers' room drinking coffee. When I told him about the story he took off the tan smock he wears for dark-room work and said we could both ride in his car.

Jones lived in a bungalow of dark maroon, almost purplish brick, with white stucco trim, and a big roofed porch. A marked cop car sat in front, and a young uniformed officer slouched behind the wheel and sipped coffee from a thermos cap. He got out of his car when Murkett and I started walking toward the front door. "Can I help you, sir?" he asked.

"I'm Al Cannon from the *Telegram*," I said, holding up a plasticized press card.

"I think they may not want to talk to reporters, sir."

"Has she got someone with her?"

"Yeah. There's a Relief Society lady," the officer said.

"I'll just ask," I said. "Thank you for your help, officer."

Murkett and I walked up to the front door. A plump, fiftyish

lady answered my ring. "Al Cannon, *Utah Telegram*," I said, trying
to slide past her into the hall. In crises people defer to police,
paramedics, firemen, doctors, anyone who seems calm, knowledgeable, and authoritative. If a reporter can seem calm, knowledgeable,
and authoritative, sometimes people will get out of his way.

Not this woman. "I don't think Sister Jones wants to talk to
anyone right now. She's had a rough jolt this morning," the woman
said. She grabbed the sleeve of my coat at the elbow and looked out
through the open front door at the officer who was standing on the
sidewalk.

"Do you know what happened?" I asked in a soft, polite voice.

"No, I don't know anything. I'm just a neighbor." The Relief
Society tightened her grip on my jacket. The officer took a step up
the sidewalk towards the porch. I turned to go. I hadn't really
expected to get in. Then a woman's voice came from inside the
house. "That's okay, Karen, I'll talk to them."

I walked into the living room. Mrs. Jones sat on a brownish
sofa. She was a slender woman in her late twenties. Her eyes were
red, but she sat up straight and seemed composed. "I'm sorry to
disturb you," I said. I squatted on the edge of an upholstered chair
opposite the sofa. Murkett stood in the archway where the polished
wood floor met the beige rug. His Nikon hung around his neck. He
looked around the room, judging the light.

"I talked to the police," Mrs. Jones said. "I had to go over it
with them several times. But it still doesn't seem real."

I waited, hoping she would continue, but she didn't. "Could
you tell me about it?" I asked.

"Well, Orson went jogging this morning before breakfast, like
he always does. He was late getting back, and I started to worry. I
didn't want his eggs to get hard, you know." Mrs. Jones's short dark
hair was damp, as if she had just showered. "It got later and later,"
she said. "I was afraid he might have fallen and hurt himself or

something. I didn't know what to do. I couldn't leave O. R. and Suzy."

"O. R.?" I interrupted.

"He's our two-year-old. Orson Randall Junior. We call him O.R., because I didn't want to name him junior in the first place." I nodded.

"Well, when it got real late, I got worried he might be late for work. I called Karen and asked her to do me a favor and watch the kids for a few minutes while I went and looked for him. Suzy was all fed and everything. Orson always goes jogging in the same place. He runs along Eleventh Avenue, then across the park by Shriner's Hospital, and then up this little canyon by the U Mountain.

"I took the pick-up. I parked it where the trail goes up the gulch by U Mountain and walked. He was just a little way up. He was lying by the trail on his stomach. I thought maybe he'd had a heart attack or something. But then I could see the blood on him, and blood on the ground around him. He was all muddy, too.

"I touched him. I knew he was dead, sort of. But I really didn't believe it. All I could think was that he was hurt and cold and I had to get him to the truck. I had to help him. I tried to lift him." Barbara Jones held her arms in a circle in front of her, right hand grasping left wrist, and she leaned back at the waist to show how she had grasped her dead husband's body and tried to lift him. "He was all slippery in front. I got him part way up, and my feet slipped in the mud, and I fell down. My hands got so slippery I couldn't hold him."

Mrs. Jones jerked her left wrist out of her right hand twice to show how she had lost her grip. She sobbed and took a Kleenex out of her pants pocket to wipe her eyes as she talked.

"There was this little hill. It wasn't very big. But I couldn't pull him up. There was this brown mud everywhere. My feet slipped in the mud, and I fell down. And my hands got so slippery I couldn't hold him." Her voice got louder and broke. "I had to leave him there. He was hurt and cold, and I had to leave him there."

The Relief Society crossed the room with her arms out to hug Barbara Jones. Murkett took a picture. The flash startled both women. They had forgotten Murkett. He took another picture. "I think you'd better leave now," the Relief Society said.

"Thank you for your help. I'm sorry to have bothered you," I said. Murkett had already turned and was headed out the door. I waved to the cop as we crossed the front lawn. The sod squished beneath my feet. It was soaked from last night's salt-smelling rain.

eight

Jones's Killer Lay in Wait, Police Believe

by Al Cannon

Though Barry Bowen commands the city desk at the stodgy *Utah Telegram*, his journalistic tastes run toward the *Police Gazette*. He loves a murder story. In his view, the Jones story was imperfect only because the victim was not female, beautiful, and scantily clad.

"Nice story, Al," he said when I came to work Friday morning. I was immediately suspicious. Bowen doesn't praise reporters as a rule. He thinks it makes them lazy. He fears a reporter who is esteemed by his city editor may spend afternoons at D.B. Cooper's while his colleagues put out the next edition.

"What do we have for a follow today?" Bowen asked. Just as I suspected, he wanted more.

"Barry, I don't cover the cop shop. I'm happy to help out in an emergency. But I won't move in on Mary Beth's beat."

"She'll do a follow. She's already got the police report. But this is a big story, Al. We need another sidebar."

"I'm supposed to cover Hastings's dinner tonight. I can't do cop stories by day and cover dinners by night."

"Al, you own this story. Readers want the Cannon touch. Do a story today, and I'll see you get some time off next week." I said I'd see. I had an idea for an easy story. Maybe I could do it quickly, get some time off today, and then call in my chit on Bowen next week as well.

I phoned the police department and asked for Lieutenant Wilford Benton. He would be running the investigation. I had known him since he was a new patrolman and I was a new reporter on the police beat. When he came on the line, I told him I knew something about Jones that might be helpful. He invited me to his office to talk. I walked four blocks to the tall, green police building. In the front hall is a booth of bullet-proof glass and a woman in uniform. She asked my name.

"Al Cannon," I said.

"Allen? Alburt? Alex?"

"Just Al," I said. She wrote it down, checked her list to see that Benton was expecting me, and pushed the buzzer that unlocked the door.

Upstairs, Benton sat behind a gray metal desk in a cramped office looking at papers. He took off a pair of reading glasses and motioned me to a chair. He wore a blue-and-green-plaid Pendleton shirt, open at the collar to show the neck of a white tee shirt underneath. I've never seen him wear a tie. Since I knew him as a cop in uniform, his blonde crew-cut has gone grayer, a paunch has grown beneath his thick chest, and his face has become wrinkled.

"Al Cannon, reporter-at-large," he said. I'd forgotten how he says that. He thinks it's funny. A framed diploma from the National

Law Enforcement Academy of the Federal Bureau of Investigation
hangs on his wall.

"What do you know about the Jones killing, Benny?" I asked.

"We issued copies of the police report to the media like we
always do," Benton said.

"I know. I read it. Do you know yet if he was shot on purpose?"

"We're not ready to issue any more statements. You can say
we're proceeding with the investigation." Benton folded his hands
on top of his neat desk and gave me a blank look. He was reminding
me I had promised to bring information.

I said, "You know Jones was working on this CalCom electric
power project. He was in charge of writing the environmental
impact statement." I told Benton about the call I'd received from
Paul Rambeau, about the meeting I'd had with Jones and what he
told me. I gave him a clip of the story I'd written about Jones's letter
to CalCom. Benton hadn't paid attention to the story before because
it didn't name Jones as the source. He put his reading glasses back
on and read the story carefully.

"Do you think this has anything to do with the incident?" he
asked.

"I don't know. It's a $10 billion project. People have been shot
over less."

Benton looked at me over the tops of his reading glasses. His
eyes were the color of faded blue denim. "Does the shooting change
anything? If Jones said they had trouble with their coal before, like
you said, then do they still have the same trouble?"

"I'd guess so. I don't know for sure. Have you talked to the
people at the Bureau of Land Management about this?"

"We talked to them, but they didn't tell us anything about Jones
holding up the CalCom project or about him leaking stories to
reporters. We'll talk to them again."

"Do you know whether he was shot on purpose?"

Benton took off his reading glasses, put the temple in his mouth, and looked at me thoughtfully. "It was a definite homicide-type situation," he said. As I said, I've known Benton a long time. He wouldn't make an explicit deal—you tell me what you know and I'll tell you what I know. But I'd given him useful information, and he would reciprocate.

"How do you know it was murder?" I asked.

"Now don't quote me saying it's murder. I don't know how the prosecutor will charge the guy when we get him, and he gets upset when I make legal judgments in public."

"Okay."

"The victim was shot twice with a shotgun, twice from two different ranges. That doesn't happen by accident."

"The police report said they weren't sure whether he was shot more than once," I said.

Benton nodded. "The responding officer couldn't make a definite determination by visual inspection at the scene. We got the medical examiner's report this morning. We know now."

Benton picked up some of the papers on his desk and looked at them. "The victim was hit in the left thoracic area with one load at an estimated distance of about twenty feet. That knocked the victim down and probably would have proven fatal. Then the assailant approached the victim and fired another load into his neck and upper back from closer range to assure the attack resulted in the death of the victim."

"How do you know the first load was fired from twenty feet?"

"That's indicated by several factors. For one, the distance is consistent with the size of the pattern. A rifle fires a single bullet. A shotgun fires a dozen or so separate pellets. The pellets fly apart as they leave the muzzle of the gun, so the further from the muzzle, the wider the pattern of pellets."

"How wide is it at twenty feet?" Benton held up both his hands, palms toward me, fingers fully spread, thumbs touching. "About like that." Then he slapped both hands high on his left side beneath his armpit and on his chest, one hand partly covering his shirt pocket. "Hit him about like this.

"We figure it spun him around, and he landed on his stomach. We don't know for sure. His wife moved the body. You know about that." Benton stopped talking and looked at me with the same expressionless face he'd used to remind me I'd promised information. It was clear he didn't approve of my reporting the sobs of new widows.

"Then he walked up and shot Jones again," I prompted. I wanted a story, not a journalism critique.

"Yeah, here." Benton turned his head and slapped his hand on the back left side of his shirt collar.

"You get any footprints?"

"Not really. Police technicians examined the scene. There were no complete impressions that could be clearly identified as the perp's."

"Why not? It rained. The ground was muddy."

Benton shrugged. "Sometimes you get them, sometimes you don't."

"You know what this sounds like, Benny? This sounds like your guys went up that gulch with four-wheel drives and made a mess of the place so you don't know whether there were footprints."

Benton nodded. "Yeah, it was hard. Mrs. Jones found her husband about 0700, something like that, and then she came running out of the canyon covered with mud and blood. She went to this lady's house . . ." He started shuffling through the reports on his desk.

"Cynthia Brownlow," I said. "She lives in the first house north of Smelter Gulch."

"Yeah, you read the report. Anyway, Brownlow calls 911, but she doesn't say Jones is dead. She says he's been hurt or something. She can't come up with details, because all she knows is this strange woman comes to her front door all bloody and in an incoherent frame of mind. So the paramedics take their truck up the canyon. They think maybe it's an emergency type situation, not a homicide. Some of the motorcycle officers rush up there too, fishtailing and having a good time getting to spin around on the dirt trail." Benton waved his hand as if shooing flies. "Don't put that in the paper.

"We got this place up the side of the hill where we think the perp sat waiting for the victim," Benton continued, perking up. "It's about the right angle and the right distance from where we think the body was discovered. Looks like he may have brought a cushion, you know, the square kind you take to a football game when you sit in the bleachers, so he could keep his bum warm while he waited to blow Jones away."

"So it was planned and calculated."

Benton nodded. "Looks that way. We think the assailant picked up his spent shells. Most shotguns eject the shells back over the shooter's shoulder. We didn't find any shells. We think maybe this guy was careful, turned his gun over, ejected the shell into the dirt at his feet, and then picked it up. That's just a guess, but it fits with not finding any shells, and with bringing a cushion and staying calm and everything."

"Would it have mattered if he left a shell?"

"Yeah, if we find the gun. We could compare the indentations in the shell butts with the firing pin on the gun. Now we got no way to prove which gun the guy used."

"Can't you tell anything from the pellets?"

Benton shook his head. "A shotgun doesn't leave any marks on the pellets like a rifle or handgun does. These pellets were number four chill, about the size of BBs that kids use in an air rifle. They're just at the large end of what hunters would normally use for ducks. We can't really tell that much from them."

"So you don't have any suspects, any motive, any footprints, or anything you can tell from the shotgun pellets," I said.

"We're working on it. We'll get him," Benton said evenly. I've never known a politician who said he would lose an election or a cop who said he wouldn't catch a crook. Benton said, "We think the perp may have known Jones pretty well or he wouldn't have known where to bushwhack him."

I shook my head. "Maybe not. I talked to Jones once, and he told me all about how he goes jogging up this gulch by the U Mountain every morning, and I didn't especially want to hear about it." Benton nodded and shrugged. I got up to leave.

"Some of this stuff is off the record," Benton said.

"What?"

"Don't say anything about the cushion. The guy might read it and dispose of the evidence." I nodded and moved towards the door. "What do you think of Barbara Jones?" he asked me.

I sat back down. He wanted to talk some more. "I don't know, why?"

"When I talked to her, I thought maybe she was holding out, you know, she knew something she was hiding," Benton said.

"I was surprised at how much she told me," I said.

"Yeah," Benton said. "Listen, you don't think Jones may have had something going on on the side, do you? That's off the record."

"Never occurred to me," I said. "You know he wore garments."

"Mormons do it, too," Benton said.

"I only talked to him once, and we didn't talk about that. What makes you think he might have?"

"Well, cutting a guy down like that with a shotgun might be something a jealous husband would do. And then I get this feeling that Barbara Jones is holding out, and messing around in something she might not want to tell us about. You know, sometimes wives don't want the people in the ward to know." Benton sighed and tilted his head to one side. "You're probably right," he said. "I asked about it at the Bureau of Land Management, and people there said Jones wasn't the kind to get involved in a crime-of-passion situation."

"You sound pretty desperate, looking for jealous husbands," I said.

"We'll get him," Benton said evenly. I sat a few seconds. He didn't seem to have anything more he wanted to tell me, so I thanked him and left.

nine

As I was writing up the interview with Benton, Paul Rambeau called me. "Listen, Al, *60 Minutes* is coming to town. I thought you'd be interested because you've been on the story."

"What story?"

"The murder of Orson Jones. I mean this is the biggest national story we've had here in years. I'm surprised the networks haven't been here already."

"Mmm?"

"This is a whole new level of disregard for the law. I mean everyone knows that the big utilities are ruthless, but murder is something entirely new. Even I'm shocked."

"Do you know something that indicates California Commonwealth was involved in the shooting?" I asked.

"Nothing you could take to

court. But it's an obvious line of inquiry. You have to ask *cui bono*? Who benefits? CalCom. They're a lot closer to getting a $10 billion project now that the one person who stood up to them is dead."

"You know, I was just talking to Lieutenant Benton about that. Do you know Benton?"

"No."

"He's the detective in charge of the case. He asked if anything had changed for CalCom. I didn't know of anything. Do you?"

"It's only been a day. Things will get a lot easier for CalCom now. Jones knew the country. He was in a position to make a difference, and he was the only one in that whole BLM office who had the guts to stand up to them. It isn't coincidence that he stops the project and then he's murdered."

"You called *60 Minutes* with this idea?"

"Yes, and they said they're interested, maybe. We really need strong press attention, Al. You know the way the establishment works around here. They'll do anything to get that CalCom plant. And the last thing they want is an investigation that could make problems for the project. You know, I hear the governor is giving a dinner tonight for CalCom. Can you imagine that? The day after the murder?"

"I can imagine it."

"You know CalCom does a lot of business in Vegas. Hiring someone down there to take out Jones wouldn't be that hard for CalCom."

"You know anything about that?"

"Well, nothing specific yet, but that would be one good place for an investigation to start," he said. I didn't say anything. "Anyway, I think public scrutiny is our only chance on this. I realize you can't do what the national media can, but I called to make sure you were aware of the situation."

"Thanks," I said. After he hung up, I wrote faster, so I would have time for a drink before I went to the governor's dinner.

ten

CalCom Acquires New Coal; Utah Leaders Boost Project

by Al Cannon

Upstairs at the venerable Alta Club, the men entrusted with Utah's destiny gathered to battle environmental extremism and invite honest industry into their state. About eighty men in wool suits, starched white shirts, muted silk ties, and shiny shoes stood laughing and talking in small groups. Among them were successful businessmen, senior partners in major law firms, leaders of press and television, presidents of three universities, and politicians of both parties. Some of these men wielded power discreetly and were known only to insiders. The fame of others filled the entire state and extended in a few cases as far as Rock Springs or Pocatello.

Waitresses in decorous black dresses with white aprons wended their way through the talking groups serving punch from silver trays. Al-

53

though the Alta Club serves liquor to members and guests, Governor Wells, eager to display his firm attachment to the Mormon church, had asked that no alcoholic beverages be served on this occasion. Such faithfulness had its reward. In one group stood a tall, spare old gentleman with withered-red-apple cheeks who said little but smiled on everyone. He was Elder Golden M. Taylor of the Quorum of Twelve Apostles, and with his presence the church tacitly blessed the proceedings.

The rumble of masculine conversation filled the room. The president of the University of Utah charmed the powerful with graceful jokes, briefly mentioning the unmet budgetary needs of his institution. A United States senator complained to a bank president of the self-serving foolishness of his colleagues in Congress. In a corner, apart from the other groups, stood five or six men from Persevere. Among them was Mayor Hafen in a shiny blue three-piece suit. He waved in recognition, and I noticed his vest parted several inches above his pants to accommodate his paunch. He walked over to talk.

"I saw what you wrote about Barbara Jones," he said. "I was just up to her place. I wanted to tell her about the talk I had with Orson. I think I told you I was going to talk to him, didn't I?"

It took me a moment to recall. "Yes, I remember you said you were going to see him right after you gave me that interview at the *Telegram.*"

"Yeah, I'm real grateful I had that opportunity. Orson and I talked about life and important things, and I wanted to tell Barbara what he said. I think it made her feel better."

"That's good," I said.

"It made it easier for me, too. You know, we were kind of upset with Orson there for a while when he come out against us on the project and everything. Only it's like when you get upset with someone you're close to. We always thought this CalCom thing would get over with one way or another and we'd get over being upset. Now we won't get that chance. So I'm real glad I got to talk to him."

"They're ready to serve," a voice said. "Would you please go to the dining room and take your seats." The voice belonged to John Kilee, a local public relations man who had been hired by CalCom. He wore thick glasses that emphasized his bulging eyes.

The mayor shifted topics while he still had time. "Say, that was a pretty good article you put in your paper about me and Persevere. I got a lot of good compliments on it."

"I'm glad you liked it."

"We need more reporting like that. Why don't you come down to Persevere and see the project for yourself?"

"You're right. I ought to do that. I'll call you," I said, sidling away. I didn't want to be roped into a long drive to Persevere.

Hafen grabbed my elbow. "Listen, we got a chamber meeting Wednesday. If you left here by six or so, you could get to Persevere in time to have lunch with us, and I'll take you out on the project in the afternoon."

"I can't do it this Wednesday, but I'll call you."

"Please take your seats. We're ready to start," Kilee said. Although the governor was hosting the dinner, CalCom seemed to be in charge.

"You'll never understand this project unless you get out and see it yourself," Hafen said. He reluctantly let go of my elbow, and I made my escape.

During dinner, I sat on the couch in the hall. A waitress brought me a cup of coffee, and I smoked and listened to the clink of cutlery and the rumble of voices in the next room. Later Jim Fox of the *Tribune* came and sat across from me. It was only a small story for him. His publisher wasn't speaking. When Governor Wells chimed his fork on his water glass for quiet, I slipped into the back of the dining room. The waitresses were serving strawberry parfait.

"Thank you all for coming," the governor said. "I think we have more Utah leaders gathered here tonight than we have ever had in one place during my administration—except, of course, at general conference," he added, beaming toward Elder Taylor seated at the head table.

Governor Wells paused and his face became sober. He assumed the Brigham Position and said, "When our pioneer forefathers came to this land, they vowed to make the desert blossom as the rose." He repeated word for word most of what he had said at the press conference. Like many Utah politicians, Wells sold insurance before entering public service. Selling insurance is good training for politics: you learn to say the same thing over and over without sounding insincere or getting tired of hearing yourself talk.

Near the end the governor made a new point. "Just this week we faced a new and potentially fatal challenge to this great, great opportunity for Utah." Federal bureaucrats had sought "to deny CalCom the Utah coal they had bought and paid for in the free marketplace." Opposed by federal might, others would have given up, "but that's not the way we do things in my administration, and that's not our Utah fighting spirit." After intensive work by CalCom and the Wells administration, a new solution had been found. Wells talked for several more minutes but never clearly explained what the new solution was. He called on Coleman Bywater to elaborate.

Bywater read a brief, dry statement. CalCom had bought new coal rights from the Westerman Development Company. The new leases were near the ones under challenge. In fact, they were part of the same formation. CalCom still believed it had valid title to the old leases and would go to court if necessary to defend its claims. In the meantime the project could proceed.

Led by the governor, Utah's assembled leaders clapped politely. They weren't interested in CalCom's coal troubles. The governor returned to the podium and said, "Bart Westerman of Westerman Development did a great job of coming through with the coal we needed to get on with this project." The governor held his hand out towards the rear, and a man with a high, shiny pompadour stood and waved to the scattered plaudits of the crowd. Then the governor called on eight community leaders each to give "a short, five-minute response." Altogether, they talked an hour and a half.

Still, for me, the evening was successful. The Utah establishment laughed at the jokes I had written for Hastings. ("Some of these environmentalists would hold up the Resurrection until the environmental impact statement was in.") And as people were milling around afterwards, Hastings shook my hand and said, "Thanks, Al, that was a real *Telegram* job." Then he moved on to mingle with his fellow community leaders.

I was just deliberating where I might go for a drink before writing the story when someone laid his arm across my shoulders and said softly, "I hope I didn't get you into trouble." It was Governor Wells. He reached to shake my hand and I smelled his aftershave and the warm wool of his suit. "You know, Al, I never complain about news stories, not even if they're unfair. But in this case I had to call Brad because the interests of Utah are at stake. You understand." The governor spoke in the mild, chiding tone a kindly camp counselor might use.

"We're always happy to hear from you at the *Telegram*, governor," I said, trying to step out from under his arm.

"Your story upset delicate negotiations, Al. It threw off our timing. . . . Isn't that a terrible thing that happened to that young Jones man?" I nodded. "It's things like that that make me glad I run a strong law-and-order administration." The governor stepped back from me in a small but dramatic gesture of recoil. "Al, that story you wrote, it had everything in it, but the most important fact."

"What's that, governor?" I said on cue.

"Why, that there's not a shred of foundation whatsoever for that letter. I talked to all the best experts, Al, and they all say it's just a ridiculous mistake. It won't hold up ten seconds."

"Bywater said Jones had a point," I said.

A perplexed frown deepened a crease between Wells's bushy eyebrows. "Yes, I don't know why Coleman would say that." The governor brightened. "Well, anyway, we've got that problem taken care of." He leaned forward as if to whisper in my ear. "Al, you can't believe the difficulty we had getting this latest coal sale through. Just between us, those regulated utilities are even more bureaucratic than state government. Now, that's off the record." I began to drift away from the governor.

"Well, anyway, I know you wouldn't harm Utah's interests just to get a news story. You're too fine a reporter for that. I'm sure it was just a careless mistake, and I wanted you to know there are no hard feelings."

The governor's blue eyes scanned the crowd looking for someone to talk to next. "'Preciate you, Al," he said and reached out to touch the president of an advertising agency. I went looking for a drink.

eleven

Across South Temple Street from the Alta Club is the Wasatch Front Club. The Alta Club caters to rich, old men escaping their wives; the Wasatch Front Club serves young men and women looking for true love, or at least an evening's sex. The Alta Club admits only respectable people approved by the membership; the Wasatch Front admits anyone willing to pay the $20 annual dues, including me. Crossing South Temple Street, I dodged a fitful stream of cars and pickup trucks, climbed a flight of stone stairs, and crossed the terrace and an interior lobby. A woman checked my membership card and wrote my name in a ledger. Inside, I peered into the smoky room looking for someone to drink with.

Bartenders in white shirts and black vests dispensed drinks from a hollow-square bar in the center of the room. Above their heads, glittering wine glasses hung in wooden racks. Elsewhere, potted plants hung from the ceiling, miraculously healthy in the smoky atmosphere. One wall was a two-story window, displaying a view of the Wasatch Mountains silhouetted against the night sky.

Across the room, near the window, I saw CalCom public relations man John Kilee just sitting down with another man. I waded towards them through the sea of cigarette smoke and palpable desire.

"Hello, John," I said.

He stared at me goggle-eyed through his thick glasses. "Oh, hi, Al," he said, and turned to the man sitting across the table. Something was wrong.

As any experienced journalist knows, a public relations man buys reporters drinks. Kilee's job was to smile, invite me to sit, buy whiskey, and in the guise of casual conversation make subtle hints as to how the story I would write later might be improved from his employer's point of view.

I tried to flatter him into proper behavior. "I thought things went well," I said, a remark calculated to set off a long discussion of the really tough decisions Kilee had faced on guest lists, seating arrangements, speaking order, and desserts, and how the governor's office took the credit but was no help at all, but that's all right because making the governor's people look good is one of the ways a clever public relations man ingratiates his client with decision-makers in government.

"Uh, yeah, thanks," he grunted. For some reason, Kilee seemed determined to shirk his responsibilities. I was tempted to go to the bar and buy my own whiskey. But of course, there was the larger good of journalism to consider, too. If Kilee were allowed to backslide with the virtual dean of Salt Lake newsmen, there would be no telling what he might try later with more junior reporters.

Trying another tack, I turned to the man with Kilee, and

recognized the high, shiny mass of his hair-do. It was Bart Westerman, the man who had sold CalCom its new coal.

"Mr. Westerman, congratulations on your coal deal."

"Yeah, thanks."

Kilee began to shoo me off, "Listen, Al, if you don't mind, Bart
and I—"

I stuck my hand out quickly to Westerman. "I'm Al Cannon. I
was impressed with how fast you were able to get the coal CalCom
needed. Usually a deal like that would take months."

"Yeah." Westerman shook my hand without rising. "Sit down."
I slid into a polished wood chair with the satisfying knowledge that
through extra effort on my part, standards would be maintained after
all.

A pretty girl with frizzy hair, who looked too young to be
working in a place like the Wasatch Front, came to the table. "Are
you ready to order?" she asked.

"Bourbon and water," I said.

"What's your name, honey?" Westerman asked.

"Julie."

"They're just making them prettier all the time, aren't they
fellas?" Westerman sprawled backwards, pushing his chair up on
its hind legs to display his masculine charm.

She managed a smile. "Would you like something to drink?"

Kilee said, "Tanqueray martini, up, stirred, not shaken, very
dry, no olive."

"Do you have Wild Turkey?" Westerman asked.

"Yes."

"Well, give me a shot. I like good whiskey and pretty women
straight." Westerman grinned again. As he leaned back, his sky blue
jacket fell open showing his western-style white shirt with white
curlicues and arabesques embroidered on it. In the dark bar it looked
luminescent.

"Bart," Kilee said, "Al here is the reporter who broke that story about the trouble the feds are giving us over our coal."

Westerman looked at me with enlarged interest. "I owe you a drink. If it hadn't been for that story, Bywater would have cheated me on our coal deal."

"Now Bart, you don't want to talk like that in front of reporters," Kilee smiled as if he were joking, but he was hoping Westerman would shut up.

"Johnny-boy, don't tell me what I can say."

"I'm not telling you what to say, Bart, I'm just reminding you who . . ."

Westerman leaned forward abruptly. The front legs of his chair thumped on the floor as he thrust his face across the table at Kilee. "Go remind Bywater. He's the one who forgets. I know he sent you over here to babysit me, but I've done my deal with him. I delivered. I don't have to take his crap anymore, and I'm not going to take it from his hired boy. And if you don't like it, I'll kick your butt across the barroom for you." Westerman gestured broadly in the general direction he would kick Kilee's butt. He spoke loudly enough to turn heads at neighboring tables.

"No, offense, Bart. . ." Kilee's voice had risen half-an-octave.

"Here we are," Julie returned with a tray of drinks.

"Put them on my tab," Kilee said. Just as I suspected, he had an expense account to entertain reporters.

Westerman reared back in his chair to get his hips straight so he could reach his hand into his pants pocket and pull out a money clip. He peeled back several hundreds and extracted a twenty. "Here, honey, we'll call it square." Julie smiled warmly, and I took the first long, cool swallow of the evening.

We sat in uncomfortable silence. Westerman was sullen, Kilee intimidated. To improve the mood I said to Westerman, "You were a hero over there. You saved the project." Westerman nodded.

Kilee said, "Bart, really, we appreciate what you've done. I mean I've never seen a sale this size pulled off this quickly in the utility business. Usually it would take months." Westerman snorted. From his inside jacket pocket, he pulled a large cigar and rolled it between his palms. "No, really, without your coal we'd have been hurting on this deal," Kilee continued. "You're mad at Coleman now, but you know he was on your side through this whole thing." Westerman put his cigar in his mouth and sucked it in and out to moisten it. Having established his right to say what he wanted, it seemed there was nothing he wanted to say.

"What do you mean Bywater was on Bart's side?" I asked.

Kilee looked at me, and I could tell he was relieved to talk with someone less threatening. "You wouldn't believe the trouble we've had over this thing. Okay, at first we wanted to buy all the coal we could. There were two holdings down there, Bart here had some and a guy named Vassos had some. We wanted to buy both. I mean you spend $10 billion on a power plant, you want enough coal, right?"

Westerman drew a wooden kitchen match from his shirt pocket, half stood, and ran the match up the back of his thigh and bottom. It didn't light. "Damn slick pants," he said. He struck the match on the underside of the table and puffed diligently. The cigar had been sweetened like pipe tobacco, and a wild-cherry odor mingled in the acrid smoke. Kilee and I both lit cigarettes in self-defense.

Kilee continued to tell the saga of CalCom. "Then management in California said we didn't need all that coal. Something to do with regulatory decisions or something. I mean, you wouldn't believe the trouble the California Public Utilities Commission gives us. They're evil."

"Yeah, and I was out," Westerman said. "They promised to buy my coal, and then they welched." Kilee winced when Westerman said "welched."

"So how was Bywater on Bart's side?" I asked to bring the conversation back on point.

"Coleman was a kamikaze for Bart," Kilee said. He ran his fingertips down his cheeks. "I mean he put on that green and black camouflage paint and tied dynamite around his waist and ran into the board of directors meeting, and threatened to blow everything up if they didn't buy Bart's coal." He nodded at Westerman. "I mean, Bart, you know, he threatened to resign if they didn't buy your coal."

"All I know is he couldn't deliver on the deal when he said he would," Westerman said.

"Why did Bywater want to buy Westerman's coal?" I asked Kilee.

"'Cause I put together a good deal," Westerman said.

"I think Coleman saw some of the trouble coming with those other leases. It turned out he was right." Kilee lowered his voice and said, "Let me tell you something off the record, okay?"

"Yeah."

"This project would be a lot further ahead, and we'd have spent less money if they'd just listen to Coleman. I mean, first, they didn't listen to him and they wouldn't buy Bart's coal here. Then even after the feds tell them they've got troubles on the other coal, they still can't make up their minds to buy Bart's coal. I mean you can't believe what Coleman had to go through the last couple of weeks to get a decision out of California. That's off the record, okay." I nodded. "So now we go back and buy Bart's coal like Coleman wanted in the first place, only now the price is higher." Kilee shrugged and sipped his martini.

"Why is the price higher?" I asked. "Same coal, same project."

Kilee said, "When we made the first deal we weren't already committed. We could say to Bart here, 'You sell at our price, or we'll move the whole project somewhere else, or maybe postpone it.'"

Westerman said, "There's no one else down there wants to buy the coal. I either sold to CalCom or I didn't sell."

Kilee said, "But now we need the coal quickly. We can't rely on Vassos, anymore. And if we move the plant, we'll have to go through the whole process of getting the state to approve the site and the environmental impact statement. If we couldn't get Bart's coal, the whole thing could fall apart."

"And that's where Bywater tried to cheat me," Westerman said, leaning across the table towards Kilee. "He didn't tell me you guys had trouble with the feds. He just said you'd decided to buy my coal at the old price. I would've sold, too, hadn't been for this thing in the paper." He pointed at me with his chin.

So now it was becoming clear. Westerman didn't owe me a drink, he owed me a lifetime supply.

"Waitress," I called. Given the size of his obligation, I intended to drink as much as I could.

"Bywater just tried to cover the whole thing up," Westerman said.

"Waitress," I called. I could see Julie standing by the bar, but her back was to me.

Kilee said, "Now come on, you've got to admit there wasn't any coverup on this thing, don't you, Al?"

"Waitress."

"Honey," Westerman said. Julie came right over. "Do it again, honey," he said, making a circular motion over the table with his forefinger.

"I'm fine," Kilee said, putting his hand over the top of his glass.

"I'll have a double," I said.

"Make mine a double, too," Westerman said. "And hurry back honey, we missed you." He slapped Julie on the bottom.

Kilee was frowning. "Al, I really want to get this straight. I mean, you know me. I always tell clients, 'You gotta level with the media. You can lie once or twice, but it catches up with you in the end.' Isn't that right?" He nodded his head answering his question as he asked it, and his eyes bulged behind his thick glasses. "But on this one, Al, even I'm scared. I mean Coleman's negotiating with Bart here for literally all the money in the world. And you come along with something you know's gonna cost us megabucks, and he just lets it all hang out. I mean you gotta admit that guy's credibility is unbelievable."

Westerman leaned back in his chair and looked at Kilee with his eyes half-closed. "All I know is Bywater kept saying, 'You got the full resources of California Commonwealth behind you,' but when it came time to deliver, he was off in California, trying to be president of the company or something, and I gotta go see the bankers alone."

"President of the company?" I said, looking at Kilee.

"Yeah," Kilee nodded. "Bywater was one of the final two for president of CalCom. People here don't realize it, Al, but Coleman's one of the most respected professionals nationally in the power industry."

"Here we are," Julie set full glasses on the table. Westerman gave her another twenty. She smiled but was careful to stand between Kilee and me, where Westerman couldn't reach her bottom.

As she left, Westerman carefully shaped his cigar ash on the edge of the ashtray and said, "After Bywater fell through on me, I had to go see this banker." He chuckled, "That dude had a poker stuck up his ass." Westerman sat up rigidly straight, raised his eyebrows, squinted his eyes and spoke in a prissy voice. "'Well, if you can't meet your commitments, Mr. Westerman, our bank will have to foreclose.'"

"I just plopped this big old envelope on his desk and said, 'There's your collateral. You can have it right now. But you better know someone wants to buy some coal. 'Cause what you got there's options, and four months from now they won't even make good toilet paper.'" Westerman chuckled. "It was worth the price of admission to see him squirm. He could see he didn't have no choice except to give me some time get a deal together."

"What do you mean you had options?" I asked.

"I gave a guy money, and he sold me an option that said I get to buy his coal at a set price for the next six months. If I don't buy in six months, he keeps the money and the coal, too."

"Risky," I said.

Westerman nodded slowly. "This business you gotta have balls big enough to bowl with," he said. He looked slowly from me to Kilee to make sure both of us properly appreciated his nerve and acumen. He drained his glass and said, "I gotta go to the little boys' room."

He walked part way across the room, ducking slightly to avoid a potted plant, then detoured over to the bar where Julie stood. He put his arm around her when she wasn't looking and whispered in her ear. She smiled but ducked away from his arm. He resumed his march to the bathroom.

Kilee looked at me big-eyed through his glasses. "Listen, Al, I'm sorry I didn't invite you to sit down before. Bart got mad at Coleman tonight, and Coleman asked me to take him out and buy him a drink, see if I couldn't cool him down." Kilee tried to sip his martini, but his glass was empty. Thinking about Westerman made him nervous. "I hope you won't print some of the things Bart said tonight. I mean it just isn't true that Coleman tried to cover up anything. You know that."

I nodded. "Why is Westerman mad at Bywater?"

"Well, first, Bart didn't get invited to the dinner tonight. We overlooked him or something, and so Bart had to call the governor's office today and ask if he could come or something like that. That made him mad." Kilee leaned towards me and lowered his voice, "Then to top it off, Coleman didn't introduce Bart at the dinner. The governor introduced him. You probably didn't even notice. I'm sure it was just an oversight on Coleman's part, but Bart's taking it like some mortal insult or something. I mean you heard him, he about took a glove and slapped me across the face and said it would be pistols at dawn."

Julie came to our table. "This will have to be last call," she said.

"Another double," I said.

"I'm fine," said Kilee.

"Bring him one, too," I said pointing at Westerman's place, "and set six back for me." I turned to Kilee, "If it was just a mistake, why didn't Bywater come here himself and explain?"

Kilee smiled sourly. "Clients don't have to explain. That's what they have me for." Then he thought better of his joke. "No, the governor asked Coleman up to the mansion after the dinner for a talk. That made things worse with Bart. He's mad because he didn't get invited." Kilee looked in the direction Westerman had gone. "You know, the way he acts, you'd think he doesn't want to be around people at all. But he's really a closet social climber."

Kilee shifted his gaze, and I turned to see Westerman approaching across the bar, his white shirt a faint, luminescent heliotrope in the dark bar. He quickened his pace as he saw Julie arrive with a tray of drinks. I reached up and took the six minis of Jack Daniels she'd brought me, and put three in each side jacket pocket.

Westerman brought out his money clip before he sat down, but this time, he peeled off a hundred, and held it so Julie could see. "Honey, we can take care of this tab real easy. You just take this, and you don't even have to go get change. You and I will just leave right now. I know where there's a party."

"I've got to stay until closing time, and I've got to check out and everything," she said. "I'll go get change," she said and reached for the bill. Westerman moved the hundred away from her and reached with his other arm to put it around her shoulders, but she backed away before he could reach her.

"It's too early to quit partying," Westerman said. "Listen, I'll just sit here and wait. I've got a brand new drink and these two gentlemen to keep me company. And then after quitting time, you and me can go find that party." He held the hundred dollar bill towards her.

Julie looked at Westerman seriously and said, "I can't go out with you tonight." Then she smiled the smile of a waitress practiced in fending off closing-time advances. Westerman looked at her and saw he would fail. He reached in his pocket, took a twenty from his clip, and handed it to Julie. She said, "Thanks," and left the table quickly.

Westerman didn't sit down. "That's all for me," he said, and turned to leave the bar. Kilee stood up. "I gotta go, Al, see you." I sat for five minutes alone finishing my drink. It's wrong to waste whiskey.

twelve

On the terrace outside the Wasatch
Front I paused and took a mini-bottle
from my jacket pocket. I breathed
deeply, and the crisp night air ran
down my throat as cool as the first
drink in the bar. A gibbous moon
lolled over the Wasatch Mountains. It
had the sky to itself. No star could
penetrate the glare of the street lamps.

Patrons straggled from the club.
A couple walked past me, silent and
untouching, her dark and curling hair
as ornate as a chandelier. The young
man looked up as he walked and blew
smoke at the moon. Below on South
Temple Street, teenagers dragged the
downtown strip, as the crackle of their
exhaust pipes and snatches of conversations shouted between vehicles
floated up to where I stood.

But the night had changed. Earlier
the stream of cars, jeeps and pick-up

trucks had seemed merely a dangerous nuisance. Now in the fresh air, the moonlight and the friendliness of whiskey, my attitude was transformed. Now young people driving in circles looking for excitement and sex made the night at once serene and promising. On such a night as this new love might prosper. On such a night as this old love might revive. There was a thought: old love might revive.

I walked to First Avenue, where I had parked my Chevette. The mini-bottles clinked softly in my jacket pockets with each step, as though I had bells on.

I drove toward the freeway, down North Temple Street, past the Mormon Church Office Building, with its two maps of the hemispheres, carved as balls in white stone on the front, and its high, white tower thrusting up between them into the night. At the stoplight in front of the copper-colored Triad Center I fetched another mini from my pocket and palmed it for a few discreet sips.

I steered south onto the I-15 entrance over the railroad tracks, past billboards, grain elevators, and a cement factory. On Forty-fifth South I left the freeway and turned into the suburbs. I drove past Dee's Hamburgers and Holiday Gas, both advertised by huge, electrified clowns, dark at this time of night; past Chuck-a-Rama and Kentucky Fried Chicken, and past a two-story brick building shared, according to the sign, by Jack Mann Insurance, L&R Realtors, and the Won Tai School of Martial Arts.

I turned onto Saffron Street and made a right onto Nutmeg. My house—or what used to be my house—was third from the corner on a block of two-story homes of frame and brick. I parked, got out of the car, and leaned on the warm fender of the Chevette. I twisted the cap off another little bottle while I surveyed the scene. Away from the lights of downtown, the sky was smattered with stars. The bowl of the big dipper hung downwards as if to pour darkness onto the State Capitol. Polaris stood unmoved over the home of Orson Jones's widow and her children, and Cassiopeia lay face down, as if her throne had fallen forward, above the U Mountain and the gulch where Jones was killed.

A breeze stirred the leaves of the cottonwood trees with a sound like rushing water. On the block, I counted four parked pick-up trucks, two with campers on their backs. In the driveway next door a plastic, big-wheels tricycle squatted like a large, horned beetle, casting a shadow along the cement driveway westward from the moon. The sidewalks and driveways of the Spice Islands subdivision were white and smooth in the moonlight.

I climbed the stoop and rang the bell. I rang again. I knocked five times in quick succession. The porch light went on. "Who's there?" a woman asked.

"Hello, Betty," I said softly.

There was a moment of silence, and then the click of metal, and the door opened the width of the chain bolt.

"It's 2:00, Al. What do you want?"

"Could I come in for a cup of coffee?"

"You're drunk, Al."

"Just a little bit," I said, grinning with all the charm a fifty-year-old ex-husband can muster in the middle of the night. "Come out and look at the moon. It shines all silvery down the sides of the mountains."

Betty shut the door. Quieter clicks signalled she was slipping off the chain bolt. I congratulated myself. I had gambled, following true to the spirit of the night to wake Betty up. She was a Mormon woman, prim and dutiful, but there were factors on my side. She loved blarney, "the moon shining all silvery," and stuff like that. And there was a time when she had loved to throw off propriety for a midnight frisk.

We fell in love one night thirty years ago when she clambered down the fire escape at Carlson Hall after the U thought all its coeds were locked up and safely asleep. At the bottom of the fire escape, a ladder would tilt slowly downward beneath a person's weight to deposit her gently on the ground. But the ladder would also set off the fire alarm. So Betty shinnied down a metal pole. I stood at the bottom, proffering advice in hoarse whispers as she climbed over the railing, and holding my arms out to try to catch her if she fell. Then we ran hand in hand across the vast dark lawns of campus, giggling in exhilaration at her escape. We stopped to pant and kiss in the shadow of the Einar Nielson Fieldhouse.

Over the years Betty became more religious and I less so. My way of living became an affront. We parted almost two years ago, I sadly, she with a feeling of relief at a hard decision finally made. But maybe once again she would succumb to a little poetry and a chance for midnight fun.

She opened the door. She didn't look as if she wanted fun. She looked like a high school English teacher who has seen all the shenanigans before and is not amused.

"I wouldn't put up with this when we were married, Al, and I won't have it now." Not a promising welcome.

I jumped off the stoop, nimble as an old dog, and stepped back out of the shadow of the house into the moonlight. I understood before I came that my act had worn thin. Yet she had not seen me for months, and, after middle-aged divorce, times can be lonely. I know that. Maybe she had softened. Maybe her English teacher's heart would consent to be pleased by moonlight and poetry. I declaimed:

> Queen and huntress, chaste and fair,
> Now the sun is laid to sleep,
> Seated in thy silver chair,
> State in wonted manner keep.

I gestured in a sweeping arc that reached its apogee toward the moon, and in its descent, paused, palm-upward, in the direction of Betty, who stood in her doorway with the lace collar of her blue flannel nightgown peeking out from the top of her turquoise robe.

> Hesperus entreats thy light,
> Goddess excellently bright.

Betty quietly shut the door and turned off the porch light. I was left standing on the front lawn, alone in the dark, my left hand outstretched in the Brigham Position. I remounted the stoop and spoke softly through the closed door. "I love you, Betty. I still love you." The wind stirred the cottonwood trees with a sound like rushing water.

I walked back to my car, noting that Betty had waited until the end of the first stanza to shut the door. She had always been partial to Ben Johnson. The moon threw my shadow before me over the white cement of the driveway. It was long and thin like Don Quixote, though in reality I am short and chubby, like Sancho Panza.

thirteen

The telephone rang viciously. I answered on the fifth ring, I think. "Cannon, where's your story?"

"What?"

"We need your story," Bowen
said.

"Oh." I struggled for composure,
and something plausible to say. I took
stock. My head hurt, but not too badly.
My tongue was fuzzy, but serviceable.
A general air of unreality pervaded the
moment, as if I were seeing myself as
a specimen through the distorting
glass of a bottle. "Put a rewrite guy on.
I'll dictate," I said.

"Al," Bowen said. He made it two
syllables, "Ah-ul," the first an octave
higher than the second. "It's after
seven-thirty. The backshop's supposed to have this already. I don't
even know how big a hole to leave.
You've got us all fouled up."

"Tell me how big you want it, and I'll write it to shize," I said. Evidently my tongue was fuzzier than I had thought. Bowen, who had been irritated, became enraged. "You picked the best night you could to get drunk and disappear. I mean this is just the publisher and the people he wants to impress most in the whole world."

"You going to keep talking, or you going to get a rewrite guy and let me get this story done?"

Bowen put the receiver on his desk with a bang. I could hear him yelling, "Barlow, take Cannon on five."

I put the phone down quickly to look for my notes. They weren't on the bureau. Probably they were in my jacket pocket. My jacket, however, wasn't in the closet. I'd probably thrown it off in the living room when I came in four hours ago. Maybe I'd left it in the car. No, there it was on the couch. But my notebook wasn't in either side pocket. That was okay. I could remember the important things, anyway. I got a beer from the fridge to help me think. "You ready?" I asked over the phone.

"Yeah."

"Utah needs the (upper case) California Commonwealth Power Project (comma) and citizens must work to bring it to the state (comma) a gathering of Utah leaders agreed Friday night (period) (graph)," I said. I took a sip of beer. This wouldn't be so hard. "Bradford Hastings (comma) publisher of the *Utah Telegram* (comma) urged leaders to (quote) get on the Utah team (that's lower case) (comma) and bring this much-needed project to our state (comma) despite obstructionist tactics of bureaucrats and so-called environmentalists (period) (close-quote) (graph)."

The story meandered through another twenty paragraphs. Hastings believes a long story is an important story, and we wanted to show him that the *Telegram* spared no pains to bring readers a full account of this important news event. As I neared the end, I laid plans to finish quickly, hang up, and leave the phone off the hook so I wouldn't have to listen to any more of Bowen's complaints. But I was forestalled.

"Barry wants to talk to you when we're finished," Barlow said well before the end of the story. I thought of hanging up anyway, but decided that would be unwise. Instead I told Barlow I had to check something in my notes and went to the refrigerator for another beer to assist me through the tirade.

Bowen came on quickly. "Al, I've talked to you before about missing stories. It's unacceptable. I'm going to let you go. You can come in Monday and pick up your check."

This was worse than I expected. I had been prepared for threats and reproaches. I had planned to drink beer and occasionally grunt in contrition. Now I would have to argue and explain. "I didn't miss a story, Barry. You've got a story."

"No, Al, this one mattered. We needed this one, and you ran off and got drunk when you should have been writing, and then we've got to take something you just rattled off the top of your head."

"Have you read the story, Barry? Have you read it? I don't know where you get this rattled-off-the-top-of-your-head stuff."

"You were drinking last night, weren't you, Al?"

"I had a drink with Bart Westerman. He sold CalCom the coal. There's a good story there, and we're going to get it first."

"Well, you're not going to do it. I'm not going to argue with you, Al. I'm not going to put up with this anymore. You're fired." He spoke in the matter-of-fact tones bosses use when they've made up their minds and want to show they're in charge.

"I don't think you can fire me, Barry."

"If you want to appeal it, you can talk to Hastings on Monday."

"I'm going to do that, Barry. But you didn't read the story. If you read it, you'll see a part that says the audience laughed appreciatively at Hastings's remarks. His speech was good. He even remembers who wrote it for him. I don't think he's going to let you fire me right now."

Bowen was silent for eight seconds. He hates to have Hastings overrule his decisions. "Cannon, I want you in here Monday at seven o'clock, on time. I'm taking you off the CalCom assignment and giving it to someone who gets his stories done."

Bowen hung up. I went back to bed, but I couldn't sleep. After an hour of lying in bed I got up and had another beer.

fourteen

**Rites Held for
Orson R. Jones**

Orson Jones's funeral was held at
noon Saturday in the North Twenty-
first Ward, where the Jones family
attended church. Before the services
Mrs. Jones and other relatives stood in
a row by the closed coffin in a room
off the main chapel and greeted a long
line of friends and comforters. I didn't
go through the line, but I looked in
through the door.

There was Governor Wells holding Mrs. Jones's hand in both of his
and bending down toward her to mur-
mur words of shock and condolence.
She looked up at the governor and
nodded her head with its shiny hair.
Then she turned away to pick up her
daughter, who looked about four and
had been tugging on the back of her
skirt for attention. Mrs. Jones touched
her nose and forehead briefly to the
little girl's face, and then set her

astride her left hip, held her with her left arm, and held out the other hand to the next person in line.

Wells straightened up and looked around to see who had been watching. He nodded to several people who were looking at him. Then, having displayed his compassion, he left by a side exit, probably, I thought, for the golf course. I wished I could leave, too. But even after a night of drinking I had come on my day off to write a story about the funeral.

In my long and checkered pursuit of the news, I have fallen into the disfavor of editors before. From experience I know that the best way to deal with tantrums, such as Bowen's, is to ignore them, work with conspicuous diligence, and soon the whole matter is forgotten. Jones's funeral presented a strategic opportunity. On Saturday afternoons, news is scarce, few reporters are on duty, and editors welcome any extra story. Bowen was out of the newsroom, unable to enforce his ill-tempered *diktat*. Work on my day off would demonstrate my devotion to the *Telegram* and in addition serve notice that I would continue to report on matters relating to CalCom undeterred by Bowen's ranting phone call that had kept me awake all morning.

An organ oozed soft music. I took a seat in a wooden pew towards the rear of the plain chapel. Seated in a loose group near the front were about two dozen people from Persevere who had made the 250-mile trip to Salt Lake for the funeral. On an aisle to the left, Merrill Gott sat with two rows full of Jones's former colleagues from the Bureau of Land Management.

Mourners filled the chapel. I slid toward the center of the pew to make room for a couple about Jones's age. The woman sat first. Her perfume smelled of lilacs. The couple and I slid inward again to make room for Paul Rambeau. It was the only time I have ever seen him wear a white shirt.

High on each side wall of the chapel was a row of narrow, gothic-arched yellow windows. They bathed the hall with light, which I am sure the architect described as golden, but which could also be called jaundiced. One of the windows bore a small cherry-colored glass inlay with an inscription: "The truth shall make you free."

A rattle like a rollerskate came from the rear, and heads turned to see two young elders pulling back sliding doors that connected the chapel with the recreation hall, where rows of folding chairs had been set up on the combination dance floor and basketball court in anticipation of an overflow crowd.

Just before the services began, John Kilee rushed in, goggled about the chapel through his thick glasses, and took one of the folding chairs. He was freshly pressed and barbered, and looked, on the day after we had been drinking, a lot better than I felt. In fact, now that I thought about it, I felt unwell. Aspirin and beer were wearing off. My head ached a little. I felt stirrings of flatulence. I wanted a nap.

At the chapel doorway a girl had handed me a small program for the funeral with a sketch of the Salt Lake temple on the front. It was daunting. There would be remarks by the bishop of the North Twenty-first Ward, two hymns sung by the congregation, opening and closing prayers, two speeches, and a duet on violin and piano performed by two young ladies in the seventh and eighth grades, who, I believe, were cousins of Mrs. Jones.

After the bishop's remarks, Mayor Hafen, introduced as "Bishop Hafen," took the podium.

"My brothers and sisters, my assignment today is to say a few words about Orson when he was a boy and young man growing up in Persevere. I was Orson's scoutmaster when he was a boy scout, and I was his bishop when he was a teenager and later when he went on a mission and got married. We saw quite a little of each other. Orson's dad died when he was real young. Orson was the same age as my boy Tracy, so he was over at our place a lot. I can still see him when he was about nine. He was a real serious boy with a lot of freckles."

Hafen spoke without notes. He held each side of the podium with his hands and rocked slightly from side to side, as if standing at a helm and gazing over mild seas. "Orson was a real special boy. He worked hard to help his mom. He was an Eagle Scout. He was one of the smartest kids they had at Persevere School. Everyone in town knew Orson was a good boy who paid attention to business and was going to make something of hisself." A violent yawn sneaked up on me. My mouth opened so wide my jaw cracked. Hangover's turn. I had been unable to sleep all morning, but now I was urgently drowsy.

"Orson loved the land. Now down in Persevere all our boys like to get out in the out-of-doors and fish and hunt and ride ORVs and that type of thing. But Orson had a special feel for the land. When he was just a boy he wanted to be a rancher and have his own land and watch it bring forth the fruits of the earth." I slipped a notebook from my side jacket pocket and began to write. For my purposes, accounts of Jones's past would do much better than a general sermon.

"Well, we all know the price of ranches anymore. I don't think there's one boy from Persevere who has been able to start in ranching, except for those who took over a family operation. Orson was smart enough to figure that out when he was still young enough to be pretty disappointed by it. I can still see the look on that young man's face when he said to me, 'Bishop, I'm never going to be able to get a ranch and settle in Persevere.' I'll tell you it was a sad day for Orson and for me, too." I stopped taking notes to cover another yawn with the back of my hand.

"But Orson wasn't the kind of boy to let a disappointment like that get the better of him. No sir, he studied hard and went to the Brigham Young University. Then he went to work for the Bureau of Land Management. Of course, the BLM's got more land than everyone else put together." Hafen looked toward the people from Persevere as if sharing a private joke. "So Orson got his land to take care of, and you can bet he took care of it just like it was his own, too."

Good. I folded my notebook and put it back in my jacket pocket. The story of Orson Jones, a fatherless boy, who was disappointed in his desire to own a ranch, but turned to federal land management where his love of the land found expression in protection of the environment, was just what I needed. Now it was time for Hafen to stop. But he didn't.

". . . serious about his education, but when the time came for me as his bishop to call him to serve a mission for his religion . . ." I would have fallen asleep, but I had no place to put my head.

"Orson got more than an education at the BYU. He met a beautiful, young . . ." Last night's liquor bubbled through my bowels. Next to me, the young woman dabbed her eyes with a white handkerchief and recrossed her legs. I sniffed the lilacs again from her perfume.

"Orson and I talked again, almost like father and son. He said, 'Bishop, I've tried to live by the principles I learned when I was growing up. Oh, I've done some things I'm not proud of, but I'm going to make things right.'" In calculating my funeral strategy, I had not reckoned on crapulence. Now I envisioned the services stretching onward into the afternoon and realized the magnitude of my error. Though I would doubtless overcome Bowen in the end, his malice would have its effect: I would suffer.

"My brothers and sisters, I bear my testimony to you that Orson Jones died at peace with God. Wouldn't it be wonderful if, when the time comes, the same could be said of all of us? I say these things in the name of Jesus Christ. Amen."

"Amen," the congregation echoed in ragged unison. "Amen," I heartily joined in. "Amen" has always been my favorite word in church.

fifteen

Early Sunday afternoon I put down the newspaper and rejected the desire for a drink brought on by thinking about what I had to do. After inspection, I chose a tie from my collection of four, put on my old-and-faithful gray tweed sportcoat, and set off to face my fate.

I drove east toward the block "U" on the mountainside near where Jones had been shot. Then I turned south, through the University campus, along Foothill Drive and the Belt Route, toward the sail-shaped face of Mount Olympus. I rolled down the window, and the mild fall wind blew away smoke from four Tareytons. I snuffed out the last, half smoked, as I pulled up in front of my brother Walt's magenta brick ranch house in Millcreek.

In the driveway two teen-age boys played one-on-one beneath a basketball standard fixed above the garage. Both of them wore the white shirts they had worn to church with the sleeves rolled above the elbows. "Hi, Uncle Al," the defense called. His brother took advantage of the diversion to attempt a hook shot. Before I could knock on the front door, it was opened by my niece, Alice, who smiled at me, showing new front teeth, which were still too large for her eight-year-old face.

In the living room my brother Walt put down his newspaper and got up to shake my hand. Walt went well with the room. His white shirt nearly matched his cylindrical lamp shades. His small-patterned tie was about the same blue as his carpet. And as he sat back on his sofa, genial, plump, and stocking-footed, he might have passed for a comfortable bolster. "Good of you to come," he said.

"Good of you to invite me."

"Yes, especially since we had to ask you four or five times to find a Sunday you couldn't wiggle out of." He smiled to show he was teasing, though what he said was true.

I called, "Hi, Suzy," to a teen-age girl in a long-sleeved cream-colored blouse who was setting the table in the adjoining dining room.

"I'm Patty."

"Sorry, Patty."

"Can't keep them straight myself sometimes," Walt said.

Both of us stood as Walt's wife LaDeena bustled into the room with both hands outstretched to me. "We're so glad you could come, Al. It means so much to us, and we just think you're special." LaDeena is small and surprisingly slender for a woman who has borne nine children. She has the brown eyes, slightly bucked teeth, and the quick, neat movements of a squirrel. "You'll have to excuse me. We're not quite ready yet." She returned to the kitchen.

Above Walt's head, the president of the Mormon church stared benignly out of a large, framed photograph on a bookshelf. Next to the picture was a bronze statuette of two hands steepled in prayer. On the shelf below, a collection of photographs showed Walt,

LaDeena, their nine children, two in-laws, and three grandchildren in various combinations. Walt and I grew up in a similarly large family. In fact, among the pictures is one of my parents' family. There I am in the back row, skinny, grinning, and crew-cut.

The front door opened, and Walt's oldest son Aaron came in. He called "hello" instead of knocking. A small boy held onto his forefinger, reaching up as a rider on a subway reaches up for a strap. Under his other arm, Aaron carried a highchair, folded for portability. Aaron's wife, whose name I always forget, followed. She carried a baby in a yellow blanket and plastic infant chair. Over her shoulder hung a red canvas bag with plastic, disposable diapers protruding from the top.

LaDeena rushed from the kitchen. "Oh, let's see her. Let Grandma see the beautiful little girl." She took the baby, infant seat and all, cooed over it and gave it back. Then she turned to the little boy and bent down, putting her hands together between her knees. "How are you, William? Are you all ready to have dinner at Grandma's?"

"No."

"Are you two? Do you show people you have a mind of your own?"

"No."

"Spencer," LaDeena called out through the open front door. "You and George need to stop your game now and come help Aaron with the high chair." Then she turned and said, "Brenda, why don't you put her in our room where it's quiet?"

Brenda and LaDeena took William and the baby. Spencer ran in from basketball, sweating slightly on his upper lip, and took the highchair from Aaron. Walt, Aaron, and I sat in the living room to talk. I asked about Walt's daughter, who is in college at BYU, and about his older, married daughter, who lives in California, and then about his son, who is on a mission in Germany.

The doorbell rang. "That's probably Uncle Moroni," Walt said.

Alice ran to answer the door, and, as predicted, Moroni came in.

"I hear they're serving dinner at this house," Moroni shouted. He dressed loud, too, in a burgundy jacket and plaid pants. He walked into the room, nodding his bald head, smiling and shaking hands. "Is that true?" he asked Walt. "Can a man get a meal in this house?"

"You bet he can, Uncle Moroni," Walt said as they shook hands.

"How are you Brother Alma?" Moroni grasped my hand with a vigor earned by eight decades of clean living, and he fixed me with a blue and piercing eye. Walt, in contrast, would not look at me at all, which was not surprising. Walt and I had an agreement that when Moroni comes to dinner I will not be invited, and Walt had not told me Moroni was coming.

LaDeena said, "We're ready to sit."

"Looks like I got here just in time," Moroni said.

As the others filed into the dining room, Walt grabbed my biceps. He stood close to speak quietly but recoiled when he smelled the leftover cigarette smoke lurking in my clothes. "I didn't know Moroni was coming until just a little while ago. LaDeena invited him, and I guess she forgot to tell me," he said.

"I wish you'd told me."

Walt smiled in a way that showed he understood my discomfort, but also saw that when viewed correctly, it was only minor, would likely in the end be good for me, and should entail no loss of humor. Walt is principal of Evergreen Junior High School, and I imagine he uses the same smile on eighth-grade boys when he refuses to let them out of algebra. "LaDeena really enjoys the discussions you have with Moroni," he said. "She says you bring out the best in him."

"Al, come sit," LaDeena called from the dining room, and she gestured towards an empty chair. "Aaron, put William here between

Brenda and me. Patty, go get the big glass pitcher from the cupboard by the fridge and bring us some water." Aaron inserted William in his highchair, brought a strap up between his legs that fastened to a seatbelt around his waist. Then he clicked a metal tray into place against William's chest. "Don't like this," William said.

Patty, Suzy, and Alice carried in platters of food. LaDeena serves the same menu every Sunday: pot roast cooked with carrots and onions, gravy made with canned cream-of-mushroom soup, mashed potatoes, string beans, rolls, and salad. "I can put it in the oven before I go to Sunday school, and it's ready when I get home," she says. When all of us were seated, Walt asked Moroni to say the blessing.

Only William and I kept our eyes open during the prayer. William twisted his neck and lowered his head until his cheek touched the metal tray of his highchair, so he could look up into his mother's face from under her bowed head. Brenda put her hand on William's shoulder.

She's just starting, I thought. She and Aaron would have four or five kids, not as many as Walt and LaDeena, but still a handful. Someday she'd have Sunday dinners like this one, with a table full of family still in church clothes. And the boys would go on missions, and the children would marry in the temple and have a lot of children of their own, and thus the church would grow and prosper in the homes of the faithful from generation to generation amidst the smell of overcooked roast beef.

"Amen," said Moroni.

"Amen," we all replied.

"Let's eat," said Moroni, and for a time people carved, passed, and dished up. "We had an interesting lesson in high priests' quorum this morning," Moroni said.

"Oh?" LaDeena said encouragingly.

"Yes. Brother Markle talked about the Word of Wisdom. He said smoking and drinking can cut a man off from the Holy Spirit faster than anything else." Moroni paused to scoop a crater in his mashed potatoes, presently to be filled with gravy. "Even moral uncleanliness."

"What do you think of that, George?" LaDeena asked.

"I guess it'sh true," George said.

"Don't talk with your mouth full," Patty said.

"I had to ansher," George said, spreading his hands before him in a what-can-I-do gesture. The sleeves of his white shirt were still rolled up in hopes of resuming the basketball game after dinner.

"Just finish the bite and then answer," Walt said.

Moroni was looking down at his plate. Light from the windows behind me shone on his bald head. Moroni's face is ruddy and wrinkled. But on his head the skin is pale, smooth, and traversed by blue veins that meander in byways and meet in junctions like a road map of rural Utah back when there weren't many roads. He looked up quickly and asked, "What do you think, Alma?"

"Don't know."

"What's that, Alma? I don't hear very well."

"Yes, we'd all like to hear," LaDeena said. "I think it helps teach children correct principles when adults discuss gospel subjects at family gatherings." While LaDeena spoke, I took a bite of roast beef and chewed conspicuously so I wouldn't have to talk. LaDeena surveyed the table for a way to nurture discussion of gospel subjects.

"Great blessings come to families from obedience to all God's laws," Uncle Moroni said. "Pass the gravy."

"Mom, Spencer keeps poking me with his elbow," Alice said. "Stay on your side of the line," she said to her brother, and she tried to impress a line in the table cloth with the edge of her hand.

LaDeena said, "Listen to Uncle Moroni, children. Some boys and girls think it's exciting to smoke and drink and use coffee and tea, but those habits can rob you of your free agency. Don't you think so, Al?"

I was about to take another bite of roast beef, but Aaron rescued me by changing the subject. "I read that story you wrote in the paper about the government guy getting shot. We talked about it down at the office because one of the salesmen knew him. What was his name?"

"Orson Jones."

"Yeah."

Brenda looked up from cutting William's meat. "It gave me the shivers to read about his wife finding him like that." She shook her head and shoulders in a simulated shiver.

"Sully was hoping he could do a deal with the guy," Aaron said.

"Who's Sully?"

"He's one of the guys who works in our shop. I think Jones was going to sell his house and move to southern Utah for his work or something."

Walt said, "Well, Al, you have an interesting job. You get out and see things."

"Yeah," Spencer said. "You get to report on murders. That's rad."

"A broken home, a scattered family—it's a tragedy," Moroni said. He looked around the table as if trying to find pieces of a broken family in the mashed potato bowl or among the remains of the roast.

"We're lucky we've been so secure here," LaDeena said. "We have a good, stable family."

"Out! Out!" William shouted.

Brenda put her hand on William's shoulder. Aaron spoke from across the table. "Be quiet, and you can get out in just a minute, son."

"Out!" William rocked back and forth in his highchair, threatening to tip it over.

LaDeena leaned over so her face was close to William's.

"Would you like ice cream? Grandma's got ice cream for good boys."

"Ice cream," William said, and subsided.

LaDeena looked down the length of the table. The ends of her teeth peeked out from beneath her upper lip. Her oversized eyes darted from me to Moroni, who was eating mashed potatoes. "We have a strong family," she reminded him.

"Look at Walter, Alma," Uncle Moroni said. "Walter sits here at the head of his family, surrounded by his seed, a leader in his community, blessed by the Lord." I looked at Walt, who was keeping his eyes on his plate. "Walter has been faithful to the church. He has followed the leaders' counsel."

Moroni pointed his fork at me accusingly. "But Alma, you have departed from the truths you were taught in your home. Your great-grandfather was an apostle. You were raised by godly parents. You are named after a great Book of Mormon prophet. Alma, if your father and mother could see you now they would be filled— just filled—with sorrow."

Moroni raised his fork above his head so it pointed at the ceiling and glinted like a beacon in the light from the dining-room windows. A dollop of mashed potatoes clung between the tines. "Repent, Alma. Return to the ways of the Lord," he thundered.

"Out! Out!" William yelled in reply.

"Mom, it's time for ice cream," Aaron said.

"Yes, let's have ice cream," Moroni said. He had repaid his hostess with an uplifting tableau for her children. He had done his spiritual duty by calling his erring nephew to repentance. He lowered his fork, as though it were an ensign and he were pausing from battle, and returned his attention to temporal matters.

sixteen

Beulah Jessup, 94

"Beulah Ann Joiner Jessup (that's B-e-u-l-a-h A-n-n J-o-i-n-e-r J-e-s-s-u-p), beloved wife, mother, grandmother and great-grandmother, died peacefully in her home at age ninety-four." The man from Larkin Mortuary dictated an obituary over the phone, and I typed it into my computer. He said he'd bring another one by later with a photograph.

Most daily newspapers have clerks who take death notices. They pay clerks less than they pay journalists. But Barry Bowen doesn't want clerks. I think that's so he can have a boring, menial, humiliating place to put out-of-favor reporters. He even made me change desks, over to obits in the corner of the newsroom. It's small and doesn't have any drawers.

"Yes, you have to sit there. It's the only desk with the obit line on the phone," Bowen said when I came in early that morning.

"There's no place for my stuff."

"Throw it away. You'll be better off," he said. I threw away a lot of stuff from my desk drawers. I was better off. The remains lay in a heap behind my chair.

"Hello, Al-babes." Mary Beth Kearney had come to console me. "I hear Barry's put you on obits."

"Yeah."

"I don't think that's fair. I heard he did it because of the piece about the dinner."

"Yeah."

"I read the piece. I didn't think it was *that* bad."

"Thanks."

"Oh, you left these at your desk." Mary Beth held out a red tie with several creases deeply embedded in it by weeks or maybe months spent in the back of my desk drawer, and three yellowing newspapers, which contained articles I had written and intended to clip for my files.

I put the tie on the pile behind my chair and threw the newspapers in the recycle bin across the aisle. "Are you moving in over there?" I asked.

"Yes, I haven't had a regular place here, because I've been at the cop shop, and Barry said I should take your desk, since you won't be using it anymore." I leaned back in my chair, and nearly fell over because it wasn't built for tilting back, the way I was used to. The new chair didn't have any arms, either. Mary Beth looked glum. "I really feel bad for you. You're a respected journalist, and Barry's treating you like you were some copy kid or something."

"Don't worry. He's been mad at me before."

"That's what I heard. They say you just wait it out."

"No, I don't wait it out. I've already begun an active campaign to get this straightened out and get back where I belong."

Kearney looked even more glum. "That's another thing, Al-babes, Barry told me to take the CalCom story. Believe me, this wasn't my idea."

"Oh."

"Don't be mad at me, Al-babes. I know this isn't fair, but this is a big chance for me. If I can do well on this one, I can sort of break into the big leagues around here, you know."

"You'll do just fine," I said, careful to keep any trace of irony or bitterness from my voice.

"Thanks a lot, Al-babes. I was really afraid you'd be mad. Listen, Barry told me to ask you for a source list and sort of brief me, you know, get me started."

I got up from my chair and bent over to rummage through my pile of displaced possessions until I found my desk directory. I read Mary Beth a list of names and numbers from it: CalCom, the governor's office, the Bureau of Land Management, and others. "Who was your source on that story about CalCom losing their coal?" Mary Beth asked.

"Coleman Bywater. You can reach him at CalCom. The number's on your list."

"No, I mean the person whose name you didn't use, the one who tipped you off about the whole thing."

"I promised I wouldn't tell the name," I said.

"No problem, Al-babes. I understand you have to protect your sources." Mary Beth looked at her list. "Could you give me some ideas where I could get started. I know it's a lot to ask, but this is really important to me, and you know more about the story than anyone."

"Well, you could talk to Paul Rambeau. He's with the Blue Sky Coalition. He says he has information linking CalCom to the Jones murder."

"No! Really?"

"Yes, I think it's partly his own thinking and conclusions, but he's a professional environmentalist. He's studied the project, and I think he's got some credibility."

"Why didn't you do the story?"

"Well, I asked some questions about it. I didn't think Bradford Hastings would like the angle."

"You think they wouldn't publish it?"

I shrugged. "You never know unless you try. Rambeau says *60 Minutes* is interested. He says they may be sending a producer to town."

Kearney's brown eyes grew large in the midst of her freckles. "I'll get on it right away. Thanks, Al-babes. I hope you're able to work it out with Barry."

"I'm taking steps," I said. She walked away, leaving me in silence, exile, and cunning.

seventeen

CalCom Wasteful, Advocate Charges

When I came back from lunch, a message on my desk said that while I was out Virginia McCambridge of CUCU had called. I didn't know her, but her number was at the bottom of the slip. It was in Los Angeles. She answered in a loud crackling voice like a boy soprano arriving at puberty.

"Yes, Mr. Cannon, thank you for returning my call. I represent the California Utility Consumers' Union. We have more than 10,000 dues-paying members all over California who support our fight against unreasonable utility rates." She paused. I waited. She continued. "I have here in my hand a copy of an article from your newspaper, entitled 'CalCom Acquires New Coal; Utah Leaders Boost Project.' It has your name on it, Mr. Cannon. Did you write it?"

"Yes."

Her voice sharpened. "Are you aware, Mr. Cannon, that my organization went to the California Public Utilities Commission just over a month ago, and we asked for some relief from the tremendous waste on this Utah project?"

"No, I . . ."

"The Commission agreed with us completely, of course, and issued a special order directing California Commonwealth not to buy any more coal than absolutely necessary for this project. Did you know that?"

"No, ma'am. This is the . . ."

"Your article says California Commonwealth is in direct violation of that order, doesn't it?"

"No, I don't think it said anything about . . ."

"Mr. Cannon, the reason I called is that, as I'm sure you know, news reports aren't always accurate, and we like to check carefully before we rely on them in our consumer work. I called to make sure that you aren't mistaken when you write that California Commonwealth is wasting all this money on this illegal coal purchase."

"Well, the story didn't say the purchase was illegal, and I don't know about wasting . . ."

"Are they buying millions of tons of extra coal?"

"That's what they said."

"That's what *who* said, Mr. Cannon?"

"Coleman Bywater. He's the . . ."

"I know very well who Coleman Bywater is. And he just said right in public, at this dinner, that California Commonwealth is buying this coal without a shred of justification?"

"No, he said it was justified. He said . . ."

"He can tell his excuses to the Commission. I just want to know if you're certain California Commonwealth is buying more coal."

"Well, Bywater said they are, and I talked to a man named Bart Westerman, who said he's selling the coal. I didn't actually see any coal."

"I see." Ms. McCambridge paused in thought for a full two seconds. Then she spoke with renewed indignation, "That purchase is illegal and without justification, and you may be sure, Mr. Cannon, that the California Utility Consumers' Union will demand that it be stopped."

Here was an opportunity to get around Barry Bowen and his peevish attempt to force me off the CalCom story. I began taking notes. "Mr. Bywater said CalCom needs the new coal if the project is to continue," I said to get her reaction.

"Look at the plans, Mr. Cannon. Look at the official plans for this project that California Commonwealth had to file with the Public Utilities Commission. I have them here on my desk right now, and they say in Section G that the expected life of the power plant is thirty years . . . wait a minute, I'll read you the exact words."

"I don't need that."

"Yes, well, the plans also say in section . . . let me see, I can't find the section right now . . . but it says the design capacity of the plant—that's the very most coal it can use—is under 10 million tons a year. I've found it now. It's in Section E." I could hear the rustle of pages turning.

"So you see, if the press would just take the time to look at the documents they show the most coal the plant can possibly use in its lifetime is 300 million tons. And just in that first coal purchase there are more than 400 million tons of recoverable coal." Ms. McCambridge's voice held a note of triumph.

"I believe I should write a story about this for our newspaper," I said.

"Why, yes, Mr. Cannon. I think that would be responsible after you've given so much free publicity to Coleman Bywater." Ms. McCambridge became helpful. She told me the date and file number of the special order telling CalCom not to buy more coal. She looked up the page numbers in the official plan that gave the life and design capacity of the power plant. And she told me the phone number of a man named Cosantino, who worked on the Public Utilities Commission staff and was familiar with the case.

"Believe me, Mr. Cannon, this is waste with a capital W. And of course, the power company will charge the poor consumers for all this coal they don't need, and of course the Commission will have to let them add a big fat profit on top of all this wasteful spending." She said "big, fat profit" with the inflection a fire-and-brimstone preacher would use to say "whore of Babylon."

As soon as she hung up, I called Cosantino. He was still at lunch. So I called CalCom in Salt Lake and got Coleman Bywater. "Yes," he said, "the Commission did restrict our coal purchases. But then after we had trouble with the original leases, we went to them and explained our position, and they gave us permission to buy Westerman's coal."

"Ms. McCambridge didn't say anything about permission from the commissioners," I said.

"She may not know about it. We appealed to the commissioners on an emergency basis just last week."

I asked about the expected life of the plant and how much coal it would need. Bywater said, "This whole thing is complicated. I think you might be our best chance to avoid a big public misunderstanding, but we can't do it over the phone. Would you be willing to meet with me informally and talk about it?"

"Yes." There was, obviously, no reason to bore Bywater with the internal politics of the *Telegram*, so I didn't tell him that I had been ordered off the story. In any case, it was a small problem I intended to solve soon.

"Could you meet for a drink?" Bywater asked. Already I could tell he would be an excellent interview. "You're on Richards Street, aren't you? Could I pick you up in front of your shop at five?"

I said that would be fine. After Bywater hung up, I sent a copy kid to the back shop for obituary page proofs. Then I tried Cosantino again in Sacramento and got him this time. He confirmed that Ms.

McCambridge's group had gotten a special order, and also that CalCom had gotten special permission to buy Westerman's coal despite the order. He even agreed to send me a copy of the file on the special order. "It's not too thick, yet," he said.

I decided I could write a story now about the California Utility Consumers' Union, and then maybe tomorrow I could do a bigger story on the interview with Coleman Bywater. Bradford Hastings would like a big story based on an exclusive interview with Bywater. As I was writing, the copy kid brought page proofs from the back shop. They gave off the metallic smell of wet ink.

It took half-an-hour to finish the story. Then I began correcting the page proofs, reading each obituary carefully to make sure the names were spelled correctly and the dates weren't mixed up, making corrections in the margins with my pen, trying to keep my hands out of the slippery, fresh ink.

"What's this, Al?" I turned in my chair and saw Barry Bowen's paunch. His light-blue shirt was bunched where it entered the chino pants at about my eye level. Though he is skeptical and pessimistic about most matters, Bowen always believes he is on the verge of a major weight loss. Because of this, he buys pants that are too small. He waved a copy of my story at me, "What's this, Al?"

"It's a story, Barry," I said.

"Al, your assignment is to put out the obituary page. It's an important assignment. We expect you to devote full time to it." Bowen spoke with exaggerated mildness, but as he spoke, he crumpled my story with one hand, his fingers reaching out in small bites to pull the paper into a wad in his palm. "We don't need you to cover funerals, or to make long-distance phone calls to consumer ladies in California. That's Mary Beth's job now. Your job is here at the obit desk." The story had now disappeared into a ball in his fist. He held it at arm's length and shoulder level over the trash can and dropped it. "Is that clear, Al?"

"I'm right here putting out the obit page, Barry," I said. I thought direct confrontation tactically unwise at this point, or I would, no doubt, have withered him with witty comebacks. Across the room I saw Mary Beth Kearney walking up to my desk—my former desk. "Mary Beth," I called and motioned her to come over. Then I reached into the wastebasket to retrieve my crumpled story, though I could have had the computer print out another copy.

Mary Beth was excited. She said to Barry, "I've got a big story. I think we may be able to scoop *60 Minutes*."

"So, Paul Rambeau worked out for you?" I asked.

"Dynamite, Al-babes, dyn-o-mite!" She gave both of her fists a little shake of excitement in front of her bosom. "Thank you so much for your help. I mean I thought you'd be, you know, angry and everything because Barry told me to take your story. But this is a great story, Al-babes, thank you."

"Anytime," I said. I handed her the story I'd unwadded from the wastebasket. "Look, here's another CalCom story that isn't bad, and we ought to do it before the *Tribune* gets it. Barry doesn't want me doing any CalCom stories, so maybe you could take a look at it."

"Oh, Al-babes, I can't do it now. I really need to get right on this Rambeau piece."

She handed the crumpled paper back, but I raised my hands in fearful rejection. "Barry doesn't want me to touch the story any-more," I said. "Still, it seems a shame to get beat on it when we have it first. Give it to Barry, maybe he can get someone else to do it."

Bowen took the crumpled paper without paying attention. It wasn't ripped, but it had a little coffee on it from a styrofoam cup in the wastebasket. "What's the story?" he asked Mary Beth.

"Paul Rambeau, he's the guy from the Blue Sky Coalition, he says he thinks CalCom may have been involved in the Jones killing," she said. "*60 Minutes* is sending a producer here to look into it."

"Well, show it to me when you get done," Bowen said. He

walked back to the city desk, carrying the crumpled story he had thrown in the wastebasket.

Mary Beth pulled a reporter's notebook from the side pocket of her blue blazer. "Al, maybe you could help me with one thing. How do you spell . . .," she riffled though a couple of pages of notes, "kooey bono?"

"Just put 'who benefits,'" I said.

eighteen

"Utah Factor is Key," Exec Says

by Al Cannon

Coleman Bywater drove up to the curb in a gray BMW and leaned over to open the passenger-side door for me. "I thought we'd go to my place," he said as we pulled back into traffic. The car smelled new. He drove attentively and didn't talk much on the fifteen-minute trip.

Bywater lived in a tall condominium on Donner Hill on the eastern rim of the valley. He parked in an underground garage that had the dusty smell of new cement. We rode the elevator up eight floors to his place, and he led me through a living room with brown leather easy chairs and a leather-trimmed bar and out onto a balcony overlooking the valley.

"Let's sit out here," he said. "It's pleasant this time of night." Over the opposite rim of the valley hung a red sun, low enough so I could look straight at it. It blazed a flamingo-colored pathway across the Great Salt Lake that pointed to the downtown office buildings. I sat in a canvas chair while Bywater fetched a bourbon for me and a scotch for himself. We watched the sun get lower and redder.

"Kilee tells me he got a call from some young woman who works in your shop. Kearney, I think her name was," Bywater said.

"Yes, Mary Beth Kearney." I don't like talking about other reporters, and I wanted to be especially careful not to say anything critical of Kearney.

"John was a little upset, in fact. He said she seems to think we were involved somehow in the Jones shooting."

"Mm," I said.

"I couldn't understand from John exactly what this Kearney woman thinks happened. Do you know?" Bywater kept his eyes on the sunset and his voice level. But he sat still and listened intently. The muscles at the hinge of his square jaw rippled.

"I haven't read her piece," I said.

"I don't believe we've worked with Ms. Kearney on a story before."

"I think this is the first story she's done on CalCom."

"Is she young?"

"Yes, but ambitious." Then to make sure I spoke well of her I added, "She's a nice person, and I think she'll do well."

"John said she got the idea from Paul Rambeau. You know him, don't you?"

"Yes."

"Do you know why Rambeau thinks we might be involved?"

"What he said to me was that CalCom was the organization that stands to benefit from Jones's death."

"Rambeau talked to you about it?" Bywater had a note of surprise in his voice.

"Yes, several days ago."

Bywater sipped his drink, and then said, "You didn't publish what he said."

"I didn't think he had much evidence." When he understood I was skeptical of Rambeau's ideas, Bywater shifted in his chair and for the first time looked directly at me through his dark-rimmed glasses.

"How does he think we benefitted?" he asked.

"He thinks you'll get the original coal leases back now. And besides . . ."

"But he knows we've already bought more coal. We don't really need the Vassos leases to go ahead," Bywater was no longer so careful to avoid showing he had feelings on the subject. He spoke more quickly and more like a debater.

"Yes, but Rambeau also thinks Jones understood something else, maybe something that could have killed the project."

"What?"

"I don't think he knows what it was. He's guessing maybe Jones understood some things better because he grew up in Persevere. And that might have made a difference if he had been one of the important officials on the project."

"One junior bureaucrat isn't going to make any real difference," Bywater muttered as if to himself. Then he said more sharply. "Did he say how we did it? Did I do it myself? Does he think murdering federal officials is part of John Kilee's public relations duties?"

"He said CalCom might have connections in Vegas. You've done business there."

"Does he have any names, details, anything more than just unsupported accusation?"

"I don't think he's putting this forward as a proven case. He thinks it would be a good direction to investigate."

"Does Ms. Kearney make it clear in the newspaper that this is just speculation?"

"I haven't read the piece."

"Yes, I'm sorry, you told me that already," he nodded. Bywater saw my drink was empty and reached for my glass. He stood up, then set the glass on a little tiled table between our chairs and said, "I'll just get the bottles," and went into the living room.

I stood up and leaned against the wrought iron balcony railing to look at the sunset. The valley had filled with dusk as a bowl fills with water, from the bottom up. The lake was now in shadow, metallic blue-gray instead of pink. On the freeways, cars had turned on their headlights. Over the top of the bowl of dusk, the sun shone horizontally, and it filled the air with such thick, red light it seemed I could lean off the balcony and float in it.

Bywater returned with a bottle of Jack Daniels for me, a bottle of Johnny Walker for himself, and an insulated bucket filled with ice cubes. "Will the *Telegram* print this?" he asked, as he arranged things on the little tiled table.

"I don't know. I don't decide what goes in the paper." I was still looking at the sunset.

"I admit I'm concerned," he said. "We expect opposition, of course. That's part of the job. But publicly accusing us of murder without any evidence does seem excessive." He stopped talking, and I looked back at him over my shoulder. He was looking downward and rubbing his forehead with the tips of his fingers. I could see his muscles work at the hinge of his jaw. "I guess I've got to call Bradford Hastings," he said. "I don't like to do it, but I think I'd better." He looked rather sad at the prospect.

I sat back down in my chair and poured whiskey in my glass. "You should call early," I said. "He gets in about 7:00, and it'll be easier if you catch him before they've planned space for the story in the paper."

Bywater took a long sip of whiskey, leaned back in his chair, and put his feet up on the balcony railing. "Did you do anything with the information that you got from Ms. McCambridge?" he asked. For him, it seemed, the serious business of the evening was over. He had made a decision to call Hastings and now he could relax. I told him about my call to the California Public Utilities Commission and the story I had written.

"Ms. McCambridge is a dedicated woman," he said. "I had hoped in coming to Utah I could escape her dedication." He smiled slightly.

"Did she run you out of California?"

"No, no." His smile broadened. "She would have liked to, though." Bywater had a wide mouth with thin lips that seemed to move with practiced ease into a wry and crooked grin now that he had relaxed. "This coal business has been a little exasperating, I suppose because we weren't prepared for it. And I wanted a chance to explain it to you." As he talked he jerked down his conservative, navy tie and craned his neck up and to the left as he undid the top button on his white Oxford shirt.

"Usually when we put up a new power station, we just buy coal from a coal company. They deliver it to the plant, and we don't have to worry." Bywater gestured with his right hand like an umpire calling a base-runner safe, but it was only half the sign, because his other hand held his drink. "This project's different. We're going to open a new mine and put the plant next door. It'll save our customers millions of dollars—tens of millions actually—over the life of the project." He swept his hand out toward the stars dotting the twilit sky. "So, of course, we're having to fight the consumers' union. They wouldn't want to make saving money easy for us."

"McCambridge says you've bought more coal than you can possibly use."

"I think she's making more of that thirty-year design life than is really warranted," Bywater said. "It's just a number for tax purposes. We say the design life of the plant is thirty years because that's how long the IRS will let us depreciate the cost of building it. After that, we'll stop taking tax deductions, but we won't stop burning coal and generating power."

Bywater looked over at me to see if I was following what he said. "That's all there is to Ms. McCambridge's complaint—in my view, at least. And I wanted you to understand our side."

"Didn't you explain about the design life to the Commission?"

"Yes."

"They didn't believe you?"

"No, they believed us."

"Then why'd they issue an order saying you couldn't buy all the coal you needed?"

Bywater smiled crookedly again. He found his predicament uncomfortable but still saw humor in it. "Well, the Utility Consumers' Union wrote several hundred letters complaining that we were buying too much coal. The commissioners didn't want to fight with consumer advocates. So they compromised. They issued a vague and general order saying we shouldn't buy more coal than we needed."

I sipped at my drink to think about that a moment. On another balcony somewhere below us came the smell of smoke and cooking meat. "Well, so you say you need both Vassos's and Westerman's coal. Why didn't you just buy both their holdings and tell the Commission you absolutely needed them."

Bywater didn't answer, and I looked over at him to see if he'd heard the question. He was rubbing his forehead with his fingertips again, running his fingers into his short, salt-and-pepper hair. "I'm a little embarrassed," he said. "I invited you here to explain about our coal, but I never thought what I'd say if you asked that question. It shows, I suppose, that I ought not to be talking to you without clearing it with John first." He adjusted his dark-rimmed glasses. "Could I tell you not for publication?"

"Okay."

He sat up straight, dropping his feet from the railing. They hit the floor with two quiet slaps. "We took the order as a hint from the commissioners. They didn't want to tell us outright not to buy all the coal we needed. That would have left them open for blame when it turned out we needed the coal and had to pay more for it. But they didn't want to rule directly against the consumers' union, either. So they issued this order suggesting that we put off buying more, and we decided that all things considered it would be better if we went along with them."

"But would waiting to buy cost you more in the long run?"

"Yes."

"Kilee told me you ended up paying a lot more for Westerman's coal than if you'd bought it to begin with."

"Yes, and it was fairly clear from the start that if we put off buying coal until after we were committed to the site, we would end up paying more for it," Bywater said, turning up both palms. "But the Commission controls our rates. They decide how much money we can charge. Getting along with them is always first priority. And the increased coal costs were something in the future, maybe decades away. Maybe we'd all be gone by the time those costs hit."

He smiled again at the ironies of his predicament. "In a way, you know, Jones did us a favor. He made us buy Westerman's coal now. If we'd have put it off longer it would have cost even more." Bywater put his hand on my sleeve. "This is all the minority opinion, you understand. The Commission won't tell you they made a bad decision to avoid a fight. And my management won't tell you they went along with the Commission even though they knew it would cost more. That's my opinion, and I'm telling you privately, and I hope you respect that."

I nodded to reassure him. "How much did it cost you?" I asked.

"What?"

"How much did it cost you to wait to buy Westerman's coal."

"Oh." Bywater took a drink of whiskey to think. "That's not been made public, but I suppose I could tell you." He tipped his head to one side, and I guessed he was thinking that he should give me new information for a story, and this was as good as any.

Bywater said, "In the first buy, we paid Vassos a bonus of $2 million dollars. We'll pay him royalties on each ton of coal produced when we open the mine. A couple of months later we had to pay Westerman just about three times as much bonus and an identical royalty agreement. He knew how badly we needed his coal. Some reporter put it in the newspaper." He kept looking straight ahead at the darkening western sky, but his wide mouth twitched wryly.

"You know," I said, "the governor, and my boss, too, say they can't understand why you confirmed that story when I called you about it. It's my job to write stories like that, but confirming it for me cost you."

Bywater shrugged. "Sometimes honesty is the best policy." He made his half-smile again, "You just need to be careful that it doesn't become habitual." He picked up the Jack Daniels to fill my glass, but I was already feeling the effects of his whiskey.

"Can I use your bathroom?" I asked.

I followed Bywater's directions through the living room. I stopped to look at three framed photographs on a white mantel over a gas-log fireplace. One of them showed a young, smiling woman in a graduation cap and gown. Another showed a younger woman, maybe eighteen, standing in front of a Tudor-style house. And a third showed Bywater with both of them against a background of rocks and pine trees.

"Are those your daughters?" I asked when I returned.

"Yes. The only thing I don't like about this job is I don't get to see them enough."

Evening breezes had begun to blow down Emigration Canyon, and they swirled and eddied around the condominium. One gust carried the scent of the barbecue. They were cooking lamb. It reminded me we hadn't eaten. I took another drink of whiskey to stave off thoughts of food.

"Kilee told me you fought the decision to put off buying coal. You wanted to buy all the coal you could while it was cheap," I said.

Bywater looked at me over the tops of his dark-rimmed glasses. "Yes, I heard you and John and Bart Westerman got together after the governor's dinner the other night," he said. The corner of his mouth twitched, and I could tell he knew we had gotten drunk, or at least that Westerman and I had gotten drunk.

"Kilee said you lost that battle within the company," I said.

"I did, and I still have the scars."

"But you turned out to be right."

Bywater shrugged. "You talked to Ms. McCambridge today. Does she think I was right?"

"She's going to the Commission to try and stop you."

"Yes," Bywater nodded several slow, just-what-I-expected nods. "I don't think she'll make much progress, though. They'll tell her they tried to do it her way, but the federal government intervened and questioned our leases, and they had no choice but to let us buy more coal." Bywater jabbed with his forefinger to emphasize his point a second time. "Jones gave the Commission the excuse they needed to do what they should have done in the first place."

"The guys you work with in the company, they can see you were right," I said.

Bywater put his elbow on the arm of his chair, rested his jaw on the pad of his thumb and extended his forefinger across his upper lip in a half-mustache. "No, I don't think so," he said after he had thought a moment. "Remember with everything included, this is a $10 billion project. The extra $4 million that it cost us to wait and buy the coal won't raise anyone's power bill enough to notice." Bywater shook his head. "No, my colleagues would stick by their decision. The first rule of running a utility is 'When in doubt, go along with the Commission.'"

The sky was nearly dark, and five or six airplanes hovered high in the southern sky or swooped below our eye level as they came in to land at the airport by the lake.

"Kilee said you were almost made president of CalCom," I said.

"He must have had more to drink than he led me to believe," Bywater said.

"He said you were one of the most respected professionals in the power business, and the project would be a lot further ahead if you had been in charge instead of the people in California," I said.

"No," Bywater pushed the suggestion away with his hand. "That's just what I need to have published in the newspapers and get back to my colleagues in California."

"Were you a candidate for president?"

"Yes, I wanted the job badly at one time."

"But you lost out?"

"After a tough fight." He turned to me and raised a finger. "You know something, though? They turned out to be absolutely right. Ever since I studied electrical engineering at USC, what I wanted to be was president of California Commonwealth Electric Power Company. But when the time came, I was the wrong man for the job. I can see it now. I'm an anachronism."

"You don't look too old."

"It's my outlook. I'm an unreconstructed engineer. I went into the power business because I knew it would grow. And I knew I could build big, efficient power stations and make energy that people could use. That's all old-fashioned now. You don't make it in the power business on efficiency, anymore. You make it on getting along. You get along with the environmentalists and the consumers' unions and the Public Utilities Commission." Bywater looked over at me. "And reporters, too, you have to get along with the reporters." I raised my glass in his direction.

"I'm not the man to do that. But I am the man to send to Utah to get this project going. This is what I should be doing." He tilted his head thoughtfully. "They thought they were just getting me out of the way. And I thought the only reason to come here was because I needed the money. But it's turned out to be just what I wanted to do, only I didn't know it."

"You needed the money?"

"Yes. Are you divorced?" I nodded. "I thought so, married men can't stay out drinking through the dinner hour."

I stood up. "I'm sorry, I didn't mean to overstay."

"No, no. I didn't mean that. I just meant that you would know divorce is expensive. I have two daughters in school, and that makes it hard to retire early." He looked up at me and made a patting motion in the air. "Sit down, have another drink. I haven't done anything but work since I've come to town, I'm really enjoying having someone to talk to." I sat down. "Maybe too much," he said.

Night had come. Double strings of yellow lamps marked the principal roads. And a myriad of unidentified lights winked and shimmered across the black valley floor. "I need this view," Bywater said. "I can't really afford this place, but I can come out here at night and no matter how bad the day has been, I look at those lights and it seems worthwhile again to be in the power business." We could hear the valley. At night it makes a faint hissing rumble, like a freight train passing far away, or the crowd at a baseball game heard on a radio.

"But they sent you here to get rid of you. What, you lost the presidency, and the loser is exiled to Utah?"

Bywater smiled, "Something like that." He motioned vaguely toward the sea of lights. "Utah has been a good place for me. In California I was just someone who couldn't change his thinking so he could keep up with the industry. But here I'm the future. I mean, look at the governor, he's so enthusiastic you'd think he had money riding on the project."

"Votes."

"Yes, exactly, people here want this project."

"Some of them."

"There's always someone against us, but a lot fewer here. The leadership is behind us. You saw that at the governor's dinner. And down in Persevere you'd think we were liberating France or something. They can't do enough for us."

In the mountains behind us night had chilled the air, and the dense air fell from the mountainsides and flowed down Emigration Canyon, swirling and gusting about the condominium that stood in its way. I buttoned up my faithful tweed jacket and held my elbows into my sides. But Bywater lay almost horizontal, his feet on the railing, his chair pushed back on its hind legs. His navy suit jacket hung down from his shoulders, and his white-shirted torso lay in the drafts. He seemed impervious to the evening chill, warmed by his enthusiasm.

"Let me tell you something off the record," he said.

"Okay."

"Back in California they don't think this plant can be built. They think the environmentalists are going to stop us." I looked over at him, and he nodded to reaffirm it was true.

"If they think it's going to fail, why are they spending so much money on it?" I asked.

"They need to show they tried. This is the best and cheapest way for us to get the power we need. If we fail here, we'll put up a series of smaller plants that burn oil or gas and our rates will go up. And when people complain about high power bills, we'll say, 'We tried to put up a big cheap plant in Utah, but the federal government wouldn't let us. You can't blame us.'"

"Like Jones's letter giving the utilities commission an excuse to let you buy Westerman's coal?"

"Kind of like that. That's a large part of utility management these days, establishing excuses for the regulators and the public." Bywater's voice betrayed only the barest trace of sarcasm. "But this project isn't going to be an excuse," he said. "It's going to be a power plant. I know something they don't. I know about the Utah factor." Bywater paused for effect. "Utah is like America used to be back when America was successful. "

"Utahns won't decide this thing," I said. "It'll be decided in Washington."

"I know that. But Utahns will have some voice, and I think they're going to carry this for us. They sent me here to fail, but I'm not going to fail. I'm going to build the biggest plant in America. I'm going to make more than enough electricity to power all those lights. I'm going to do it in an environmentally responsible way, and I'm going to do it cheaper than anyone else can get power these days." He bent his legs so his chair rocked forward on its hind legs, and he raised his glass. "Building well is the best revenge," he said.

I drank to that.

nineteen

Preparations were well laid; the time had come to strike. The next morning, despite after-effects of Bywater's Jack Daniels, I was in early. When Bowen went into his morning meeting with Hastings, I phoned Mayor Hafen in Persevere. "Are you having your chamber of commerce meeting tomorrow?" I asked.

"You bet, every Wednesday. Why don't you come down? We'll take you out on the site, show you why we need this project down here."

"Well, I'd like to come. Are you going to be talking about the project?"

"You bet. Anymore that's about all we talk about down here."

"Well, let's plan on it. I'll try to come. If I can't, I'll call, and we may send another reporter."

"It's about a five-hour drive, so you'll have to get off early if you're going to eat with us. And plan on spending the afternoon, so we can show you around."

"Where will you be meeting?"

"We'll be eating at Ida's this week, but listen, why don't you just meet me at my place. It's the Persevere Penneysaver, first chance to buy gas right as you come into town."

"Thank you, Mayor." I rang off.

I walked across the newsroom and stuck my head in the door where Bowen was sitting in front of Hastings's desk. "Excuse me for interrupting. I just talked to Mayor Hafen from Persevere. They're having a meeting of the Persevere Chamber of Commerce tomorrow at noon. They're going to discuss the CalCom Project, and the mayor invited us. I thought maybe you'd want to send a reporter."

Hastings looked up and smiled. "Come in, Al. In fact, we were just discussing the CalCom story." His forearms rested on the front of his bare and shiny desk, and he held several sheets of paper with perforated edges where they had run through the computer printer. He set the papers down and straightened them into a neat pile. "What about this meeting?" he asked.

I sat in the empty chair next to Bowen in front of Hastings's desk. I said, "Businessmen and community leaders in Persevere are going to discuss how the CalCom Project will benefit their town. And the mayor said that afterwards, he'd take me—or whomever— out to the project site and show us around."

Hastings stared into space over our heads. I looked to follow his gaze. It rested on *Iraqis Crushed, Kuwait Freed,* the headline he looks to when making bold decisions. "Well, it's a commitment of our travel resources, but this is an important story. I think we should go, don't you, Barry? This is a chance to find out what the top people in Persevere are doing."

Bowen nodded. "I'll tell Mary Beth." He swiveled his head and glared at me. He is suspicious of me in general, and now he suspected specifically that I was trying to get off the obit desk and back on the CalCom story. His look said he was not fooled by my tricks, and he was not going to let me off.

"She'll have to leave early. It's about 250 miles," I said.

Bowen nodded. "We can talk about it later," he said. He looked over at me again to warn me that it would be disloyal to go over his head and appeal my exile to Hastings.

"Barry, do we really want that little girl on the road for that long?" Hastings asked.

"She can do it," Bowen said.

"I told them we might send another reporter." I looked from Hastings to Bowen to make sure both noticed how cooperative and unselfish I was.

"This is Mary Beth's story," Bowen said.

"That's another thing I wanted to ask you about," I said. "I got an exclusive interview with Coleman Bywater last night, and I wanted to know if you wanted me to help Mary Beth do the story or just forget it."

"What did Coleman say?" Hastings asked, sitting up a little straighter in his high-backed, black-leather swivel chair.

"He believes the project has a good chance of succeeding—"

"Well, that's real news. We'll stop the presses for that one," Bowen said.

"And he says it wouldn't work anywhere but Utah, because Utahns have a strong work ethic, and they want to grow and prosper. He says the Utah factor is what will make the project succeed." I raised my voice to talk over Bowen's feeble sarcasm.

Hastings slapped his desk. "Now that's a real *Telegram* story!" he said. "That's the kind of work that will show readers we're on the Utah team." He made a fist and punched the air.

"I think we ought to get both sides," Bowen said.

"Well of course, we'll get both sides. Can you get it in today's paper, Al? We want to beat the competition on this one."

"I think I can. I'd need some time to work on it."

"We can put you on special today, can't we Barry? I think we should put this on A-1, don't you?"

"We'll see how it turns out," Bowen said.

To return to the subject of the Persevere trip, I said, "Hafen says people in Persevere don't trust most of the news media. They think the Salt Lake media give only the environmentalist side. But they trust the *Telegram*. They were really impressed with your speech at the governor's dinner," I said to Hastings. "Hafen said that's the kind of support they hope to get from Salt Lake."

"That's another thing, Barry," Hastings picked up the sheets of paper lying on his desk. "I wonder if this Kearney girl has the seasoning for this CalCom story. I told you about the call I got from Coleman Bywater, and frankly when I read this story I think he has a point. I'm afraid that she might reinforce that negative stereotype of the Salt Lake newsman in Persevere. Don't you think so, Barry?"

"No, we'll brief her. I think she can do a good job." The roll of fat above Bowen's collar was turning pink. This conversation was not going the way he wanted.

I nodded in agreement and looked at Bowen. "Tell her not to call the project 'the big belcher' down there," I said.

Hastings's eyes darted from me to Bowen and back again. "You were the one they invited, weren't you, Al?"

"Yes, but that's just because I've interviewed the mayor before, and he thinks I understand his point of view."

Hastings pursed his lips. "Barry, you know that we don't interfere in running the newsroom. That's your job, and we give you our full support. You and Al have your differences, and we're not going to intervene in that, and Al hasn't asked us to." He held his palms up appealing to both Bowen and me as reasonable men to judge for ourselves if what he said wasn't correct. I nodded solemnly, to show I couldn't have said it better myself. "But Barry, we think that it might be better for the *Telegram* to send Al on this story to Persevere, don't you? I mean, we're not taking anything away from this Kearney girl when we say we don't know if she can deal with the sensitivities down there."

Hastings picked up the printout on his desk. "She didn't do very well with this story Coleman complained about. She gave entirely too much space to this radical environmentalist . . ." He looked at the sheets.

"Paul Rambeau," I said. "Well, we can't find his name here right now." Bradford Hastings was still looking at the sheets. "Paul Rambeau," I said.

"Anyway, I think considering the sensitivities, we should send a more seasoned reporter, and Al is the one they invited." Bowen said nothing. Hastings smiled at Bowen to show how he supports his subordinate managers and how he was glad to see that we could all cooperate for the good of the *Telegram.*

Later as I sat at the obit desk typing a story based on the Bywater interview, Bowen came and stood by my desk. "I've got to have you on obits today, Al," he said.

"Hastings told me he wants this interview with Bywater," I said.

"I know, but I don't have anyone to put on obits. You got to stay on obits today. I'll try to spring you tomorrow."

"I've already arranged to go to Persevere tomorrow. I'm not even coming into the paper. And if I do obits today, I don't know when I'll get this interview with Bywater written up." Bowen looked at me sternly. "We can go talk to Hastings right now and see which he thinks is more important," I suggested.

Bowen's stern look vanished. He didn't want to go back into Hastings's office. "Al, look, I just don't have anyone else today. Help me out will you?"

I sat back in my chair and looked up at Bowen. "Tell you what, Barry," I said, "I'll cover obits for you today, and I'll stay late and get this other story written up, too. But then I think I should get back on the CalCom story regularly, don't you?"

"Okay, Al, I'll see if I can do that."

"And while I'm on this trip to Persevere, I may take an extra day. I think there may be a good story in Price on coal."

"Okay, Al." He walked back to the city desk.

I sat at my word processor, wily, straight-faced, and victorious.

twenty

**"Project Can Save
Persevere,"
Leaders Say**

by Al Cannon

As one of the most senior and respected reporters at the *Telegram*, I can usually avoid getting up early and driving long distances for a story. Most mornings I get up late and find a story within walking distance of my apartment. Younger, more eager newspeople vie for assignments on the road and happily traverse mountains and deserts to bring back accounts of a murder in Kanab or a cricket infestation in Vernal. But my journalistic practice emphasizes insight rather than effort, and focuses on downtown Salt Lake City. In battle, however, exertions are unavoidable, and Barry Bowen's insults to my professional standing at the *Telegram* constituted a *causus belli* that demanded energetic countermeasures.

I began the long journey to Persevere before sunup, when the sky looked like gray flannel and my left eye stung from lack of sleep. I headed south. Along the length of the Wasatch Front, a long string of cities and towns suckles up to the streams flowing from the Wasatch Mountains like a litter of piglets suckles up to a sow. Once again, I reflected, experience and cunning had overcome Bowen's brute authority. I yawned, and raised my eyebrows as high as I could in an effort to stretch my eyes open against sleep. Somehow I was unable fully to savor victory.

After sixty miles of freeways and towns I turned east up Spanish Fork Canyon out of the cities and into the mountains. The highway shares the narrow canyon bottom with the Spanish Fork River and the D&RG railway. Only a few canyons lead to passes that make it over the Wasatch Mountains to the outside world, and all of them are well trafficked. The rising road turned my face upward into the rising sun. I thought how Orson Jones had jogged into the mountains when the morning was cool and the sun hadn't yet found the gully bottoms, and someone lying in wait had killed him with a shotgun.

The road climbs up the canyon bottom for twenty miles then slithers between mountain peaks onto more gently rising sage-brush-covered hills. Near the summit, the carcass of a deer lay beside the highway. As I passed, two black-and-white magpies strutted away from the body, and then quickly circled back as their hunger overcame their alarm.

Over the broad summit, the highway plunges down Price Canyon. The road and the rail line curve in parallel with the muddy Price River. Around one bend the canyon widens to accommodate the Castle Gate coal mine. Ramps lead from the mountainside to large, metal sheds painted a uniform yellow-brown. Piles of coal lie on the ground, and a high tower bestrides a rail spur and loads coal onto gondola cars. Price Canyon opens into Carbon Valley. The road becomes four lanes and skirts the coal and railroad towns. I would come back and stay in Price that night to interview coal promoter Nick Vassos in the morning. That interview would tighten my grip on the CalCom story against any future attempts by Bowen to pry me off.

The road descended again out of coal country and into the desert. Unlike the red-rock deserts of southern Utah with their alien grandeur, the central Utah deserts are barren and ugly. The dirt is brown-gray and nearly naked. Flat-topped mountains with wrinkled rock faces and aprons of talus fallen around their ankles watch over the road from the distance. The land looks old and sick. The canyons, plains, plateaus, and deserts go on entirely too long. Utah would be improved if someone could do geological surgery and cut a couple of hundred miles out of its middle.

Eventually I reached I-70 on its course from Denver to Los Angeles and drove the uncrowded freeway before turning south again into red-rock country. The dirt turned the color of tomato soup, spotted with the soft green of cedars and juniper trees. Red buttes rose on both sides of the winding narrow road. Persevere showed first as a row of poplar trees shaped like skinny feather dusters standing against distant blue mountains. It was the first town since coal country 140 miles back. Billboards sprouted touting the Red Rock Motel, Bruhn's Family Restaurant, and "Persevere, Gateway to Scenic Utah."

Persevere Penneysaver was the first business to greet visitors on the outskirts of town. There were two gas pumps and a small cinderblock building sporting a faded sign of a smiling Scotsman with bagpipes and kilts. I pulled up to the self-service pumps to buy gas from Mayor Hafen as a gesture of good will. He came out of the glass door wearing a straw cowboy hat and a smile. He took the gas nozzle from me and adjusted it in the hole.

"You're just in time," he said. "Lunch'll start in about fifteen minutes." He grabbed a squeegee from a bucket and washed my windows. "Come on in and meet Susan," he said, as he hung the nozzle back on the pump.

Inside, the mayor's wife sat on a stool at the cash register. Her face was plump and pleasant, and she had brown hair going gray and cheeks the color of the red rocks. She shook my hand. "We're so glad you came all this way to get our side. We kind of feel the media just prints what the environmentalists tell them and don't pay any attention to us." She smiled to show she was friendly despite her complaint. Near the checkout counter a machine oozed Big Icees, and two glass pots of coffee steamed next to styrofoam cup dispensers in three sizes.

"Your children in school?" I asked as I paid for the gas.

She nodded, "We just have the three left at home. Then we've got one on a mission, one at the Y, and two others have moved away."

"So the ones at home help you with the store?" I said.

"You bet. They take turns most nights. And they can mind it all day Friday and Saturday."

"Aren't they in school on Fridays?"

"No, the district had to cut back. It's good for us with a family business, but it's hard on some families."

"We got to go or we're going to be late," Hafen said.

"Well, give us a good writeup so we can get the plant, and my kids can move back home," Susan Hafen said.

"I'll try," I said.

The mayor pushed the door open for me and said, "Park around back. We'll go in my truck, if you don't mind being seen in it." He drove the battered, green pickup slowly past the Persevere Merc., Hollywood Home Videos, Rexall Drug, and the Egyptian Movie Theater, which had a "cl sEd" sign on the marquee. Between businesses, old houses still stood on Main Street that looked as if they dated back to the founding of the town. They were made of large adobe bricks, a little darker than the surrounding red dirt, with picket fences and tall cottonwoods or willows in the front yards.

The mayor braked for a four-way stop sign in the middle of

town. On the far corner was a two-story brick building with a red stone entryway facing the corner at a 45-degree angle. "Bank of Persevere" was carved in a sandstone slab over the doorway. The mayor parked by the bank, and we went into Ida's Cafe next door. "We alternate Chamber lunch every week between Ida's here and Bruhn's place down the street," the mayor said.

The Persevere Chamber of Commerce filled three round tables in the back of Ida's. The mayor introduced me around, but I only remembered the names of the people who sat at the same table I did: Merl Tanner, chamber president, who ran the Red Rock Motel; Heber Hanson, a rancher, who said he just came to meetings when he wasn't real busy; Rulon Crowe, the banker, the only man besides me who wore a city-style coat and tie; Ervil Taylor, the barber and county commissioner; and Floydeen Jarvis, who owned the beauty salon.

As soon as we sat down, the waitress came to pour coffee. Rulon Crowe and Merl Tanner turned their cups upside down. Hafen was talking to Heber Hanson about deer hunting, and the waitress started to pour coffee for him, then she stopped and said, "Oh, I'm sorry, LaVar, I forgot." She moved the mayor's cup over by me and filled it. Hanson said to the waitress, "You don't sell nearly as much coffee as you used to since they made LaVar bishop," and he grinned wolfishly, showing teeth so large, I was sure they'd been capped. Everyone at the table chuckled, including the mayor. Taylor said to me, "Even some of us Mormons down here have a cup of coffee. It's not frowned on like up in Salt Lake." He looked past me at Hafen, and his upper lip twitched into a grin again at such a good joke. "LaVar used to drink coffee until they made him bishop and he had to quit." Taylor's large upper lip had a deep central furrow, like a rabbit's, and his lip twitched into a grin again at such a good joke.

The waitress returned with plates of meatloaf, mashed potatoes and gravy, and carrot buttons. Jarvis said, "Ida, meet Mr. Cannon here. He works for the *Telegram* up Salt Lake, and he's down here to get the real facts on the project." Ida was a bulky woman in a brown uniform with her hair in a blonde bun. She finished setting down the plates, wiped her hands on her apron, and offered one to me. I stood as I took it, not gracefully because my legs were under the table, and my left hand had to hold my napkin in my lap. "Thank you for coming," she said. She smiled nervously and added, "Excuse me, I've got to rush today to keep up." Beads of sweat dotted her upper lip.

Jarvis leaned towards me across the table as I sat down. "Ida and me are the only women members of the chamber. But she waits tables when we have lunch at her place to handle the business. So I'm the only real acting woman member today." She smiled and her blue eyes glinted. She was about my age, but still had a pretty woman's confidence.

Hafen said, "Al here came to find out about the project, and we ought to tell him a little about it."

For a moment, no one spoke. We could hear men talking about deer hunting at the next table and the clink of forks on plates. Crowe said, "Well, I can tell you it's crucial for the economy of this area. If we can't capitalize on this opportunity, then I honestly don't know if our economy can remain viable." Crowe had narrow shoulders, a narrow face, and fleshy nose. He peered nearsightedly across the table.

"Ranching's in trouble, uranium's gone, power plant's about the only chance we got right now," Tanner said. He looked about forty, the youngest person at the table, and also the biggest, with blonde hair combed flat sideways across his head and a pink face that looked as if he didn't have to shave.

I asked him, "Environmentalists say the plant would hurt the tourist business. Would it hurt your motel?"

"No." He shook his head. "Be good for the tourist business. Get us some new roads, some traffic through here, just what we need."

Taylor said, "We got plenty of room for both the tourist industry and the plant. That's what some of these outside people don't understand is how much room we got down here. You take Utah just south of I-70. We got more land than Massachusetts and Connecticut and Rhode Island put together. Lot's more. We can put the power plant out on that plateau, and tourists won't even know it's there, hardly." He sniffed and twitched his upper lip, "Once the environmentalists get over complaining about it."

Hafen said, "I think the CalCom people were pretty careful to pick a place for the plant where it wouldn't spoil any scenery. Coleman Bywater himself came down to approve the site. You remember that, don't you, Merl?"

Tanner said, "Yeah, Bywater and them drove around in that big red Cherokee they brought up here from California, a real nice vehicle."

Crowe said, "Our economy can't really function on tourism alone. We have five national parks and a national recreation area in the southern third of the state, and our poverty rate is more than double the national average. Tourism alone can't support a vibrant economy."

"Well, you're sure doing your part for a vibrating economy," Hanson said. "You loaned all your money to out-of-town coal speculators." He made another wolfish grin.

"Is that why I couldn't get a loan for my real estate office?" Jarvis asked, looking at Crowe. She didn't smile. Crowe sat silent, erect, and serious, his nose jutting before him like an ensign. He reminded me of Charles DeGaulle.

"How is your real estate business doing, anyway, Floydeen?" Hafen asked.

"Well, I got your listing, and one from Ervil. And I just got one yesterday from Kimball Whittle. We got plenty of listings. All we need now's some buyers moving in."

"I didn't know the Whittles were moving," Hafen said.

"I think they just decided it's too much for them," Jarvis said. She turned her wide cheekbones and blue eyes at me, "I took the real estate exam up Salt Lake and got my real estate license. I think real estate's going to do real good when the project comes. And I've got lots of experience running the beauty parlor. It's been real successful." She smiled again.

"Hair business is always good business. People got to eat, and they got to get their hair cut," said Taylor the barber.

"You got land for sale?" I asked the mayor. He nodded and kept on chewing. I had caught him in mid-bite.

Jarvis said, "All those people who come with the project, they'll have to have someplace to live and everything. LaVar's offering twenty-two acres that would make a real convenient mobile home park, and Erv's got a lot that's zoned commercial."

"So you'll make some money if the project comes?" I asked the mayor.

"Hope so," he nodded, still chewing.

Hanson said, "We're all hoping to make a little money. I've been scratching along here all my life. This here's a chance to make it finally amount to something."

"Do you want the plant just because it will make money for you?" I asked.

No one spoke for a moment, and then Taylor said, "If we don't get it, I think we're all washed up. We lost 20 percent of the people in this area in the last census. Look around the room here. We're all older folks. Our young people are all leaving. We gotta get something in here or we won't make it."

"You can't make it on cattle and tourists the way you always have?" I asked.

"They're driving me right out," Heber Hanson said in a matter-of-fact voice. "They've cut my AUMs down to where I can't hardly make it anymore."

"AUMs?" I asked.

Hanson looked surprised. It didn't occur to him that anyone wouldn't know what an AUM was. "Animal Unit Month," Hafen said. "The BLM leases us enough range to feed one cow for one month, or they used to."

"Now they're trying to raise my fees 500 percent and the environmentalists say they don't want any cattle on the range a'tall. They want me run out of here entirely. I got to find me a new line of work."

"Seems like the federal government owns all the land, and they just don't want us here anymore," said Tanner. "We could of had two other power plants before, but the environmentalists wouldn't let us. And they won't let us have any development on Lake Powell, hardly. They won't let us graze on the range. They won't let us develop our coal." He wiped up the last of the gravy on his plate with a piece of white bread. "If they don't let us have something, we can't make it."

"If we can get this one project, it will bring a lot of prosperity to this whole region," Crowe said. "Just this power plant would pay fifty times as much taxes as the rest of the county put together. We could cut taxes, open our schools up for a full five-day week again, build roads. A lot of new people would move in. Our economy would grow."

I said, "That's another thing. Some people say growth won't be all that good for the town. They say you'll have a lot of newcomers, and maybe some of you'll make money in the short run. But the newcomers will live in trailers and want bars to drink in, and Persevere will turn into a boom-town, like Rock Springs or Gillette, and your lifestyle will change."

"Could use a little changing," Taylor said. "Maybe we could get a bowling alley."

"Erv and his wife like to bowl," Hafen said to me.

"Only reason I ran for the county commission," Taylor said. "Those meetings go on. It's worse 'n church." He shook his head.

"But I got to have some excuse to drive that far every week. Don't seem worth it hardly, go all that way just to bowl." He stretched his upper lip into a grin at his own predicament.

"Maybe we could get the movie theater to open back up, too," Jarvis said.

"If we could get a bowling alley, I'd quit the damn county commission," Taylor said. Ida came to pour more coffee.

Crowe said, "We may find our priorities are out of order. We've been worrying too much about our environment and not enough about our productivity. Ten years ago, our country was the world's biggest creditor nation, and now we're the world's biggest debtor, and if we don't start producing more energy, and manufactured goods, we could face economic . . ."

"They find out any more about who shot Orson?" Hanson asked me.

"Not that I know of," I said. "I talked to the lieutenant in charge of the case last week. They think someone ambushed him."

Jarvis looked as if she might cry. "Orson was such a nice, gentle boy. That was such a terrible thing for anyone to do."

"We saw the article you did after you talked to the lieutenant," Tanner said. "The whole thing's stirred up a lot of interest here, Orson being a local boy and everything."

"I think he was gunned down by some of them eco-terrorists," Hanson said.

"Why would they do that?" I asked.

"Orson wasn't radical enough for them. Oh, he went off and joined the BLM and everything, but he was repenting of that, wasn't he, Bishop?" Hanson looked at LaVar Hafen, and grinned with his big teeth again. Hafen took a bite of mashed potatoes.

I said, "The environmentalists I talked to said Orson was their hero. He challenged CalCom's coal leases, and they think he might have stopped the whole project, if he had lived."

"Yeah, well I don't think it takes a whole lot to start them shooting, anymore. I saw where a couple of them got blowed up with their own bomb in California. They was down here shooting my cattle, and they put sugar in the gas tanks of some of them cats over on the Burr Trail," Hanson said.

"Did you lose cattle?" I asked.

"Three head."

"They sure yours were shot, Heber?" Mayor Hafen asked. He kept his eyes on his plate.

"Well, Wade thinks maybe they was lost or rustled. No, I don't know for sure."

"Wade's the sheriff," Ervil Taylor explained to me.

"But they shot eighteen head over Escalante," Tanner said, "found the carcasses and everything."

"They ever find out who did it?" I asked.

"No, never did catch them," the mayor said. "Don't know for sure it was radical environmentalists."

"It was them, all right," Hanson said.

Hafen stared at the middle of the table and said, "I think it's only a few of the environmentalists who are for violence, and I don't think even most of them would shoot anybody down cold-blooded, the way Orson was shot."

Jarvis said, "You know, though, they come through town, and some of them are so dirty, and they act so ignorant to you, and some of those girls, I don't think they ever get their hair done."

Tanner looked at his watch and said, "We got to talk business for a little bit."

He tapped on his water glass to bring the meeting to order, and they talked about efforts to attract a doctor to live and work in town. I looked over the notes I'd taken during the talk about the project. Other than a gravy spot on one page, they were legible.

twenty-one

"It's just got to be too much for Kim, anymore," Nancy Whittle said. She stood with the the mayor and me in her front yard by the "For Sale" sign. A boy looked at me from behind her leg. His hair was white-blonde and his stomach stuck out between his shirt and diaper.

"I can understand that. It makes a long commute," the mayor said. He had told me he just wanted to stop by the Whittles for a minute before we went out to the project site, as he had just heard at the Chamber lunch that they were moving. Nancy Whittle had greeted him warmly, "Hi, Bishop Hafen," and shook my hand when we were introduced.

She wore a red plaid shirt, Levis, and high-topped jogging shoes. Her light-brown hair was gathered in a careless ponytail, and in front the bangs hung nearly into her eyes. She looked about the same age as Orson Jones's widow. "He says there's lots of work there, so he can stay close and come home every night," she said.

"That's good. You shouldn't have to be away from each other so much," the mayor said. Across the yard another boy, maybe five years old, was riding a rope swing tied to an apple tree. A breeze stirred and carried the cidery smell of overripe apples. I could see fallen apples, brown and rotting, in the lawn under the tree. Bees crawled on them.

"Kimball's a good father," the mayor said. He reached down to pat the little boy on the head, "You've got a good dad," he said. The little boy ducked behind his mother, where the mayor couldn't reach him.

"Mommy, watch me," the older boy called from the swing.

"I just wish it was any place but Las Vegas," Whittle said. "I worry about the kids. There's so much there that just isn't wholesome, you know?"

"Mommy, look," the boy called from the swing.

"The church is stronger in Las Vegas, anymore," Hafen said. "There are a lot of good people there."

"That's what Kim says. He says there's a real nice ward and it's close to the mobile home park."

"Mommy, I can touch the branches," the boy called. He pointed his toes at the apple boughs, and in fact he was daring for a boy of five. I turned to watch him. He leaned his head back and fell forward through the arc, and I could feel in my stomach the rush of the swing, and imagine the maze of silvery-green apple leaves above his face and the blue sky shining through.

"That's pretty high, all right," the mayor called to the swinging boy. Through the branches of the apple tree I could see a neighbor's barn. The walls of unpainted wood, weathered gray, didn't reach to the roof, and a stack of hay showed through the gap. A brown horse loafed in the barnyard, sticking his head over the fence, maybe in hopes the boy would feed him an apple.

Whittle bent over to pick up the smaller boy who had stepped from behind her leg and raised both arms asking for a pick-up. "I just feel so much better here, you know. We have our families and the ward and everything, but I guess we'll make out. I guess we'll have to." She smiled gamely.

"Sister, if you live the gospel, your boys will grow up just fine," Hafen said.

"That's the main thing," Whittle said. She looked at me uneasily, not certain she wanted to talk about religion and her home in front of a stranger.

"We're going to miss you, sister," the mayor said and touched her lightly on the shoulder, unembarrassed by my presence. In fact, I guessed he took the time to visit Whittle partly to show a reporter her distress.

twenty-two

**Site Hides Plant,
Backers Claim**

by Al Cannon

"I keep telling Erv the county's got to fix this road," the mayor said. He negotiated his pickup along a narrow strip of pot-holed blacktop that wound past red mesas and over hills of pink dirt scantily covered with sagebrush. "He says they don't have the money. But if they can get this project moved along, maybe they can talk CalCom into prepaying some sales tax or something and use that to fix the road." The mayor swerved into the left lane to avoid a hole in the pavement. "CalCom people are going to need a better road than this to get out there," he said.

"How far is it to Vegas?" I asked.

"About 300 miles. A little over five hours." After a moment he added, "Kimball Whittle's a good man, but he had some bad luck." The Whittles had stayed on the mayor's mind as they had on mine. "He was driving cat on a job down by Lake Powell," the mayor said, "and while he was on break someone drove the cat into the lake. Wasn't his fault, really. But he got fired." The mayor tilted his head to one side and raised his eyebrows behind his dark glasses.

"Way things are now, only work he could find's in Nevada," he added.

"Ever find out who did it?"

The mayor shook his head. "The sheriff thought it was maybe environmentalists, but I don't know. Maybe it was just kids playing a prank." He shrugged.

The mayor slowed down to cross a narrow bridge over a dry wash. "We been losing families pretty steady," he said. "It's kind of like the Indians." I looked over at him; he kept his eyes on the road. I could see the passing pink hills reflected in his sunglasses. "I mean my great-granddad and them came here, and drove the Indians out."

He quickly took his right hand off the steering wheel and held it up towards me. "I don't want to say anything against the pioneers. They were good people who did what they thought was right. But the Indians had their own way of life here, and it got destroyed." The mayor paused and swallowed. "Now the same thing is kind of happening to us. Our way of life here is being destroyed by the government and the environmentalists." The mayor glanced over at me sneakily, past the corner of his glasses without turning his head.

"The Whittles want to stay in Persevere with their folks and live the way we do in Persevere. And they could do that, no problem, if the government would let us mine coal and graze cattle and do what people do everywhere else in the country to make a living. We'd be fine. We aren't asking for welfare. It won't cost taxpayers any money. We just want to be able to work and make a living."

"But you have to use the government's land to do it," I said.

Hafen nodded. "It used to be just part of the way we lived here.

We grazed cattle on public land or prospected for uranium or drilled for oil or whatever. But anymore, the environmentalists complain, and the news media listens to them, and the government looks at us like some kind of problem they really wish they didn't have to put up with.

"If things keep up the way they are, our way of life is going to go away just like the Indians. Our kids are going to end up living in Las Vegas or California or something like that, and it isn't what they want to do or the way they was brought up, neither." He raised his eyebrows and tilted his head, "Nothing much I can do about it, except tell Nancy Whittle her kids'll turn out all right if she keeps the commandments."

The paved road ended. A track climbed in switchbacks up the side of a red mesa. The mayor said, "CalCom already had to hire a grader and get out here and do some work on this road up the mountainside here." He shifted down. "Last time I was here was with Coleman Bywater and his CalCom staff. They had this big new Cherokee they drove out from California. But they couldn't hardly get it up the hill, even in four-wheel drive. One place, just up here a little ways, we had to stop and get out and roll some big old rocks off the road."

The mayor smiled and shook his head. "I was afraid Bywater'd get mad at the road and call the whole thing off. But he got the grader out here, made this road a whole lot better." The mayor's mood improved as he talked about improved roads. The higher switchbacks led us back through the dust we'd stirred up on the lower levels. It drifted in through the open windows. I could taste it. Red dust, bland and gritty, probably contained a full recommended daily allowance of iron.

"Look at that coal seam," the mayor said. He pointed out the window where coal showed dusty black between two layers of red sandstone. "You can see another outcrop over there." He stopped pointing to use both hands to turn the wheel fast around a hairpin curve. "The seam runs under the whole plateau. It's fifty feet thick in some places. It's low-sulfur, too. Won't pollute as much as eastern coal," he said.

The road meandered across the top of the mesa, past bare rocks longer than city blocks and taller than buildings, past sagebrush, cedar trees, and clumps of scraggly grass turned golden in the early fall. I asked, "What did Jones say to you the last time you talked to him? Did he really say he repented joining the BLM like Heber Hanson said?"

Hafen drove for a moment in silence. Then he said, "I think those are Heber Hanson's cattle." He pointed through the windshield at a half-dozen white-faced cattle munching amber grass on a hillside. "Yeah, those are his, you can see the block-H brand."

"Will he have to move them if the plant gets built here?"

"Don't see why. I think they'll stay out here same as before. Course the BLM might run him off whether the plant comes or not."

"This BLM land?"

"It's all BLM land. We been on BLM land since we left town twenty-five miles ago."

"What'd he mean at lunch when he said Rulon Crowe loaned all his money to outside coal speculators?"

"What?"

"What did Heber Hanson mean at lunch when he—"

"Oh." The mayor nodded and concentrated on the road. "Well, I don't know for sure," he said. "And I think if it's okay with you, I won't speculate. With the press and everything."

"I noticed you changed the subject very smoothly at lunch when Heber and Floydeen were asking Rulon about it."

"Well, it's Rulon's money, and where he loans it's his business." The motor rushed as the mayor geared the truck down and bucked it across a little dry wash. I braced myself in the seat with one hand on the dashboard and the other against the top of the open window frame.

"I think right here's where the old CalCom leases start, right on this drainage," the mayor said.

"What do you mean, old CalCom leases?"

"The coal leases they bought from Nick Vassos, the ones they started with. I think they had rights to mine the coal below the surface starting about here."

"Where are the leases they bought from Westerman?"

"They start a few miles down the road," the mayor nodded as if pointing ahead with his hat brim.

"You know Vassos?"

"Some. He's been down quite a few times over the past ten years or so. Probably knows more about this coal field than anyone who isn't a geologist."

"Westerman been down?"

"Not that I know of. First time I ever heard of him was the governor's dinner." An overgrown, two-wheeled track branched off to the right. "There's an old mine down that road," the mayor said, pointing. "Someone spent a year or so in there during the energy crisis in the '70s when coal prices went up. Then they went bust."

"I hear a lot of people went bust trying to mine this plateau."

"Yeah, it's a local joke about outsiders coming in to get rich off coal. There's been a dozen mines go broke up here." The mayor looked out across the red hills and rocks. "The coal's there, and it'd seem like a man could mine it. But once you get it out, you got to truck it a 140 miles to a railroad. By the time you do that you can't hardly make it pay." The mayor nodded. "We got the right outfit this time, though. CalCom won't move the coal. They'll burn the coal here and move the power. CalCom's got plenty of money behind them to make it work." After a moment he added, "If the government'll let them do it."

The truck pulled over a hilltop. "There's the site," he said. Below us was a white one-story building and a semi-trailer without a cab. We bumped down the hill, and the mayor pulled up next to the white ready-made structure. A sign read "Utah Project California Commonwealth Power Company."

Behind the building were mounds of red dirt and pink rocks, pushed up by a bulldozer that had levelled a place for the office and the trailer. Uprooted cedar trees stuck out from the piles at ungainly angles. We got out of the truck. The air smelled of dust, sagebrush, and diesel fuel.

"You can see they're testing the wind," the mayor said. He pointed to the top of the trailer where a silver anemometer spun like a weathervane. "They got another station with one of those up on that ridge," the mayor said. I peered up at the ridge following his finger, but I couldn't see the other station.

"There's a meteorologist staying in Persevere and he comes out here a couple of times a week to check the instruments. Lets up weather balloons, too," the mayor said. "They need to have a real good idea of how the winds blow out here so they'll know where the smoke'll go."

"Where will it go?"

"Well, there won't be a whole lot." Hafen took two steps backwards so he could point past the trailer. "You can see the notch in that ridge? They'll bring the pipe right across there, and bring a lot of water in here from the Green River. They'll use that for their wet scrubbers, and they'll take out over 99 percent of the pollution before they let anything go up the stack." He looked up at the sky. "Then they'll build big tall stacks to disperse all the smoke they do emit, so it won't show up anywhere."

"Some of it'll get to the parks, won't it?"

The mayor nodded curtly. "It won't be much, and I don't think anyone'll even be able to notice it. But anymore, you ask people around here whether they'd rather have the plant or the parks and they'll tell you the plant."

A distressed look came over his face as he realized that wasn't what he wanted to say in the newspaper. "Not that we don't value the parks. That's really what I wanted to show you here, Al, these people are doing a real careful job."

He swept his finger at the surrounding ridgelines. "See, we're in a kind of depression here. They put the plant here because the ridges will sort of hide it. You won't be able to see it hardly until you're right on top of it."

"Except for the tall stacks."

"Yeah, you'll be able to see the stacks." He looked at me slyly. "How many people you seen since we left Persevere?"

"Haven't seen any."

Hafen nodded. "That's right. This isn't exactly the Grand Central Station of the whole tourist industry. No one comes here, hardly. This plant isn't going to bother anybody. Now, I think the mine mouth'll be over that direction at the base of that hill. And they'll transport the coal right to the plant by conveyor."

"Underground mine?"

"You bet, won't be one of those great big strip mines rips up the whole plateau. You won't hardly be able to see the mine. They're even going to bring in top soil and plant grass on their tailings piles."

"Did Jones really repent of joining the BLM?"

The mayor looked at me a second with his mouth open. "I talked to Orson as his bishop, and I don't think it's right to tell you or anyone else what he said." He looked away from me. Then he added, "I'll tell you this though, he didn't repent of joining the BLM. That's just Heber Hanson's idea of a joke." He turned and walked a few steps towards the office building. A scared lizard scuttled away from him, and then froze.

The mayor turned back towards me. "Orson was kind of like my own boy, you know. I guess I still get upset real easy when I think about him." He looked contrite. "I can't tell you what he said. But I can sure tell you he was a fine, young man." The mayor took off his hat and rubbed his hand back from his forehead over the top

of his head, grieving, angry, and trying not to be. The shadow of his
arm moved across the lizard that was hiding like a stone on the
ground. The lizard thought his enemy had found him out, and
scampered off again to hide under the temporary white office
building.

twenty-three

After 45 Years, Coal Man Hits Deal of Lifetime

by Al Cannon

Nick Vassos sat in a booth at Corky's Cafe explaining to me how years of study and effort in the energy business had finally made him rich. "Finding coal's the easy part," he said. "Utah's got coal like a barnyard's got manure."

He was a plump man with fragrant hair. A thick ring topped by what looked like a gold nugget sparkled on the middle finger of his right hand as he raised his cigarette to his mouth. A smaller ring topped with a gold coin from a foreign land winked from his pinky. A gold chain secured a gold nameplate to his wrist. "Finding someone who wants to buy your coal, that's the hard part," he said.

Corky's Cafe was nearly full. Coal miners in bill hats and tee-shirts lined the counter. Businessmen in open-collared shirts filled the booths,

144

sharing coffee and conversation before work. One slender, dark-haired, fortyish woman in Levis and cowboy boots went from table to table greeting people as if she were running for office.

"How long have you been in the coal business," I asked.

"About forty years," Vassos said, "forty-five years if you count the time I spent underground." I wrote that down in my notebook and took a sip of coffee. Vassos said, "I went to work in the mines when I was fifteen. Had to lie about my age to get on. After a while I got smart and figured out dealing leases was easier than mining coal."

His wavy white hair had streaks of iron gray. He had two, three, or four chins depending on how he held his head. He wore a crisp, white shirt with the sleeves folded back to show sturdy forearms. Gray chest hair spilled out his open collar like a bouquet.

"Ever had a deal like this before?" I asked.

He shook his head. "I've had some good ones, but never one big as this." An elderly waitress in a yellow polyester pantsuit brought eggs scrambled soft and links for me, and bacon and eggs for Vassos. Her hair was the color of cantaloupe.

I was hungry. I'd left Mayor Hafen at the Persevere Penneysaver at sundown, driven 140 miles to Price, and arrived late and so tired that I went to bed without supper. I was glad the meeting with Vassos was for breakfast. "How long did you work on this deal?" I asked, and I ate instead of taking notes.

"Fifteen years, I guess. Long time, anyway." He shook the ketchup bottle over his slab of hash-brown potatoes. "Mostly I bought leases from guys on the plateau who went broke. And I hung on to them. Paid the government the money you have to pay every year to keep coal leases, did the work you have to do. Kept me broke."

"Did you borrow from banks?"

Vassos looked up from his ketchup bottle just as it started to pour. "Banks don't loan on coal leases. Too risky. If CalCom hadn't come along when they did, I'd been dead. Pretty soon, the government's not going to let you hold leases anymore. I'd lost my coal and my money and fifteen years of work. No bank's gonna lend on coal leases." He looked down and noticed he had a lot of ketchup on his potatoes, set the bottle down, and put the lid back on it.

He said, "You want a bank loan, you go into the shoe business or something. Coal's for guys can stand a risk."

"Where'd you get the money then?"

"I got investors."

"Who are they?"

"They prefer to remain anominous." I looked up from taking notes. Vassos's eyes were on his plate, busy with food. I could see his fat was added onto a stocky, muscular body—a strong man in a working-man's town.

I asked, "Did you know this deal would work when you started fifteen years ago?"

"No way to know for sure what'll work and what won't."

He spread grape jelly on a slice of white toast. "I could see there was coal there. I knew California's gonna get more people, so they're gonna need more power. I knew they can't build coal plants in California no more, so maybe they're gonna wanna build one in Utah." He nodded and shrugged at the same time as he reached the conclusion of his reasoning: "If I put a package together, maybe I can sell them some coal."

"Why can't they build plants in California?"

"Clean-air rules're too strict."

"If they won't take the thing there, why should we take it for them here?" I asked.

"Money."

"Well, you got some of it," I said.

"A little."

"I heard your bonus was $2 million dollars."

A look of irritation passed over his face. "Yeah, I saw where you put that in the paper. Bywater told you. It was supposed to be confidential."

He gestured around Corky's with his fork. "It was the talk in here for a couple a days. Now everyone of these guys knows my business." Vassos sounded as if they'd slept with his wife.

The crowd at Corky's is different from the morning cafe crowd elsewhere in Utah. Price is populated by Greeks, Italians, Slavs, and Czechs who came to mine, instead of Mormons who came to farm. The look of Main Street and the atmosphere in Corky's are like a mining town in Montana or Wyoming that somehow got plunked down as an island in the middle of Mormon country.

"You know Bart Westerman?" I asked.

"Yeah, sure. He bought leases from me."

"The leases he sold to CalCom, he bought from you?"

"Yeah."

"How did he do that?"

"Made me an offer."

He used his toast to push egg and potatoes onto his fork while he talked. "He came along when it was clear the government wasn't going to let us hold leases much longer, and it looked like the CalCom deal might be off. He offered enough for part of the package so I come out all right even if I didn't make a deal with CalCom."

He picked up a slice of bacon with his thumb and forefinger and took a bite. "Seemed like a good deal at the time."

"What made you think CalCom wasn't going to buy?"

"Bywater told me the big shots in California didn't really think they could make the project work, and they might give up on it." He picked up his coffee cup, then held it with both hands with his elbows on the table. "He told me that in confidence. Said he could get in trouble if anyone found out he told me. But if he can't keep my confidences, I'm not keeping his." He sipped his coffee and put the mug back on the table.

"Then Westerman offered to buy?" I asked.

"Yeah."

"You know where he got his money?"

"All I know's his check was good."

"He paid all at once by check?" I asked.

"Yeah, he wanted me to carry him. Pay me later. I told him that's not the way I sell coal. I want cash now."

"How much did he pay you?"

"That's private information."

"You sorry now you sold?"

Vassos shook his head. "Not really. I'd've made more if I'd've hung on. But I made money, he made money, we both come out all right."

"But he got a $6 million bonus. It doesn't make you mad that he comes into the deal at the last minute and gets the big money?"

"If I got mad everytime someone else made money, I'd never be happy." Vassos used his last piece of toast to wipe egg yolk from his plate. I had been taking notes, so I paused to shovel in the last of my breakfast.

I said, "You know CalCom planned to buy both your leases and Westerman's together right at the beginning. They wanted all the coal they could get. But then the California Public Utilities Commission told them not to buy so much coal and so they only bought your leases."

"Yeah, I know all about that."

"When they had to choose, why did they buy yours instead of Westerman's?"

"I had a better package. I kept the best stuff."

"Did Westerman know you were keeping the best coal?"

Vassos thought for a moment and shook his head. "I don't think so. He really doesn't know that much about the coal business." He saw I was finished eating, pulled an unfiltered Camel from his shirt pocket, and squinted his fat cheeks up around his black eyes as he lit it. I lit up too.

"The BLM going to ruin the whole thing for you by declaring your leases invalid?" I asked.

"No." Vassos leaned toward me in the booth, resting his elbows on the yellow Formica table top. "Those are good leases," he said. He looked straight at me as if contradicting his legal opinion on the leases would be an insult to his character. "That kid who said they're no good don't know nothing about coal. I been in the coal business longer'n he's been alive."

"But Coleman Bywater said that Orson Jones had a point. Maybe they won't let CalCom have them."

Vassos shook his head. "Bywater had no business saying that. Soon as I saw it in the paper, I went up Salt Lake and told him." Vassos blew smoke as though it were directed at Bywater.

He said, "All it is is just that one kid. When the higher-ups in the BLM look at what he done, they'll change it back."

"If CalCom didn't get the leases back, would it cost you money?" I asked.

"Maybe." Vassos flicked his cigarette over the ash tray as he gathered his thoughts. "My deal works like this: I got the bonus, and then I get a royalty on every ton of coal they produce. So if they go ahead with the project, and they use my coal, I stand to make some money."

"Except Jones's letter could cost you that money."

"Yeah."

"How much is it?"

"I told you already, I keep my business private."

"Is it more than your bonus?"

Vassos let smoke drift out his nose. "It wouldn't come all at once like the bonus, it'd come some every year. But it'd add up."

"So you figure Jones's letter could cost you millions of dollars if you don't get it overturned?"

"Yeah, but I'm not worried," Vassos said. The waitress with cantaloupe-colored hair came to clear away the dirty dishes. I asked for the check. I had to get on the road if I was going to be back in time to get a story in today's paper.

twenty-four

CalCom Gets Disputed Coal

by Al Cannon

As I was writing the story about Nick Vassos, Barry Bowen walked across the newsroom and stood by my desk. "Is this anything?" He handed me a press release from California Commonwealth Power Company.

It said: "Coal leases held by California Commonwealth for its Utah Project have been tentatively approved by the federal Bureau of Land Management. In a letter to CalCom, BLM state director Merrill Gott said, 'After further review, questions concerning the validity of certain coal leases purchased by California Commonwealth have been resolved.'"

I said, "It's a story. I'll get you something short right away and try to get a full piece for the late edition." Bowen walked away. I read more:

"Mr. Gott added that approval of the leases in no way constitutes per-

151

mitting the planned California Commonwealth Utah Project. 'No final decision on whether to permit the project will be made until after completion of a full environmental review process,' he said. Coleman Bywater, director of the Utah Project said, 'We're pleased with this decision. It is a major step towards successful . . .'"

I stopped reading and called Paul Rambeau. "Have you heard the BLM changed its mind and gave CalCom back its coal?" I asked.

"No? Really?" He was silent a moment. "What did I tell you? Didn't I tell you this was going to happen? I predicted this exactly."

"Yeah. You got a comment?"

"Yes. Yes, I have a comment. This is a bad decision. An illegal decision. And the Blue Sky Coalition will go to court if necessary to get this decision overturned. This shows how big out-of-state corporations can bend government to its will against the public interest. We believe the people of Utah will demand more from their government in Washington than to bend over . . . don't say 'bend over,' say 'cave in' . . . cave in to brute money power and ignore the best interests of this and of future generations. We think—"

"Wait a sec, let me catch up." I typed his words into my processor.

"Can you believe that, Al? Murder for electricity and profit. And so far they're getting away with it."

"Uuh," I was still typing more than listening.

Then Rambeau asked, "Do you know what happened to Mary Beth's interview with me?"

"They decided not to run it."

"Oh." Rambeau was quiet while I typed. "Well, I'm not really surprised." I started reading over what I had typed. "But isn't that just what I've been saying, Al? Jones stood in the way of this plant." His voice warmed to the way facts fit his theory. "He gets murdered, and now suddenly everything's smooth sailing for CalCom. And Al," he paused for dramatic effect, "the establishment is making sure no one looks too closely into the makings of this particular sausage. Isn't that right?"

"Yeah. Listen, while I got you, let me ask you about the proposed location for the plant. Mayor Hafen says the location will hide the plant, so it won't interfere with the environment. You got a comment on that?"

Rambeau snorted, and for several minutes explained to me why the location was no help, and proper policy was not to build the plant at all.

"Are you coming on the trip?" he asked.

"What trip?"

"Oh, we sent a press release, but I guess they didn't give it to you. We're going to take a busload of media down to southern Utah to show them how the plant would damage the parks, and in fact the whole ecosystem. Tom Brokaw said he was interested in coming. Lanny Barrington will meet us down there and explain some of the things."

"How'd you get Lanny Barrington?"

"She's a real environmentalist. She knows a lot about this issue."

"Yeah, I'd like to come."

"I hope we can get Tom out here. We need some real media investigation of this mess."

"Thanks, Paul. I gotta go." We rang off. I took out my phone book, and in the blue government pages I looked up the number of the Bureau of Land Management. I asked for Merrill Gott. The receptionist sent the call to his office, but when his secretary found out who I was, she sent the call to Jack Hampton in media relations. He confirmed what the press release said. "Yeah, Al, we sent the letter to CalCom, and they've got the leases, for now at least."

I asked if I could get an interview with Gott. Hampton said he'd get back to me. I typed a five-paragraph story quoting the news release and Rambeau. Just before I finished, Kearney came over and stood a short distance from my desk.

"Hi," I said.

"That turned out not to be such a good story you gave me," she said. She was subdued and reproachful.

"Mary Beth, I've never given a really good story to another reporter in my life," I said.

"You set me up," she said.

"No. Be fair. You asked for a story idea, and I gave you one. I warned you Hastings might not like it."

"Yeah, you did. They say you always get around Bowen. You always get your stories back."

"If I couldn't get around people like Bowen, I'd have been out of this business years ago," I said.

My phone rang. It was Hampton from the BLM. He said Gott was free, and he'd talk to me now, if I could come over. I told him I'd be there in five minutes. I was glad to talk to Gott and glad to get away from Mary Beth.

twenty-five

"No Dark Conspiracy," BLM Boss Says

by Al Cannon

When I arrived on the seventh floor of the Federal Building, Jack Hampton was waiting for me in the hall by the door to Merrill Gott's outer office. Like me, Hampton is fiftyish, but unlike me, he is rangy and tan. He has a lean face and hawk-like brown eyes. He says he works for the BLM so he can get outdoors. He led me past two secretaries into the inner office. "You know Al, don't you?" he said to Gott as we entered.

Gott was sitting behind a desk that looked like a kid's log cabin playhouse. The top was smooth, but the sides were logs rough-hewn with an axe; half the bark was left. "Appreciate you coming over, Al," Gott said, as he stepped out from behind his desk to shake hands.

His chair was made of cattle horns: two long ones bent downwards to form an oval frame for the back of the chair, and within them three pair of horns stuck out of a tooled-leather column as if from a cow's forehead. All of the horns were polished and arranged so they wouldn't poke the sitter. Gott himself looks like a weathered, wiry cowboy painted by Remington. He parts his graying brown hair just above his left ear and combs it over the top of his balding head.

"Is that comfortable?" I asked, pointing at the chair.

"Wouldn't have it if it weren't," Gott said. He smiled, I think. It was hard to tell for sure. "You know, the trouble with a career here at the BLM is you get into it because you like to work outside on the land. But as soon as you get a little seniority they lock you up in an office. Isn't that right, Jack?"

"You bet," Hampton said.

Gott gestured at his desk and chair, and smiled, I think. "Helps me keep the walls from closing in," he said. There seemed no danger of the walls closing in on Gott. He heads the Bureau of Land Management, which controls almost half the land in Utah, and his office shows his importance. The upper half of two walls are banks of windows that look down on State Street and the Federal Reserve Bank.

He led me to a corner of his office where we sat in calfskin wing chairs. Hampton sat on the couch. "That was a quick turn-around on CalCom's coal leases," I said.

Gott smiled, I think. "We put this on an expedited track," he said. His rumbly baritone dropped into the bass register. "I mean, Al, you've heard the bad rap we get here in the public service about how we're slow, and we can't make up our minds and all we do is churn paper." He moved both hands in overlapping circles.

"But, Al, on this one, I've just got to confess I'm proud of the people we have in this agency. The governor challenged us to resolve this issue fairly and quickly, and the people in this office rose magnificently to meet that challenge. Isn't that right Jack?"

"You bet," Hampton said. He was staring past us out the big windows so intently, I turned my head to follow his gaze. All I could see was blue sky and one wispy white cloud.

"Let me tell you something, Al," Gott said. "I don't mean to be critical. We understand the rights of the media here, don't we, Jack?"

"You bet."

Gott leaned towards me in his chair. "But, Al, if you hadn't run that story about Orson's letter when you did, we'd have had this whole fuss solved a long time ago. We were all set to go, when you ran that story. In fact, we'd have had it solved before CalCom had to buy that extra coal."

"Really?"

"No doubt about it. We were ready to go. In fact I told the governor we were ready. I don't think he would have had his announcement if he hadn't thought we were ready." Gott looked away and lowered his voice. "That's one of the reasons he was so concerned, when he saw your story about Orson's letter in the newspaper."

Gott leaned back in his chair and spread his hands. "Of course, after the issue became a public controversy, we thought it prudent to consult with our people in Washington, and that held us up a while." He waved away the lost time with a brushing motion, then pointed his finger in my general direction. "Al, I can see you don't let much get past you as a reporter. First question you asked here was right on the story."

"I heard the governor put a lot of pressure on you," I said.

Gott tilted his head back and looked at me with his eyes half shut and his mouth half open. His lips were thin, his upper lip arched, which made his partially open mouth scimitar-shaped. "No, there wasn't any pressure."

"I heard the governor came here a couple of times, and that he was angry and demanded you overrule Jones's letter," I said.

"I'm not going to comment on any private conversations we may have had with Governor Wells," Gott said. "Other than I will note that Bureau policy calls for constructive interaction with appropriate state authorities, and our interface on this issue was entirely within those guidelines." He ran his hand over the top of his head from left to right checking his combover.

"If it wasn't pressure from the governor, why did you overrule Jones?" I asked.

"I don't think it's entirely accurate to characterize our action as overruling Orson," Gott said. "We clarified some parameters on the issues he raised. His letter never really went through our decision-making process here."

"Jones said Vassos's coal leases were speculative and government policy is to discourage speculation. He was right, wasn't he?"

Gott nodded. "Orson was a talented young man, and the issues he raised were real." Then he leaned towards me. "But CalCom isn't holding those coal leases speculatively. CalCom has every intention of opening up a mine and putting those resources to beneficial use." He stared at me to make sure I understood his point. Then he leaned back and said, "The decision-making authority considered the issue in a broader frame of reference and decided the CalCom applications meet the criteria for an affirmative leasing process."

He raised a cautionary finger. "I must emphasize the decision is tentative within this timeframe. The question, of course, is whether the entire proposed use is appropriate at that location. We can answer that question better after we've completed the environmental impact statement, which we're preparing at this time. We made that clear in the letter, didn't we, Jack?"

"You bet." I looked at Hampton. He was staring out the window like a caged hawk longing for the sky.

"If Jones raised real issues, why did you take him off the environmental team for the project?" I asked.

"I didn't . . . I don't think that's an appropriate way to characterize our action." Gott ran his hand over the top of his head again. "Orson and I talked it over and decided he would take another assignment."

"Doing what?"

"We hadn't fully delineated which tasks he would assume." Gott looked at me, and his mouth took the shape of a scimitar again. "Did Orson tell you how I changed his assignment?" he asked.

I was surprised he knew that Jones and I had talked. I didn't know what to say, and sat silently. Gott smiled, I think. "Could we go off the record?" he asked.

"Yes."

"You'll remember right after you talked to Orson, Governor Wells called you?"

"Yes, he tried to get me to kill the story."

"Well, he called me right after he talked to you, and he was, ah, a little upset. We're off the record now," he reminded me.

I nodded.

"He didn't know how you'd learned about the letter, and I didn't, either," Gott said. "As I told you, this office had made great efforts to get this issue resolved."

I nodded again.

"So after I talked to the governor I confronted Orson, and he admitted he had talked to you and told you about the letter. I guess he could have lied about it, and I would have believed him, but he told the truth." Gott looked down at the sheepskin rug at our feet. "I can still see him. It was obvious he felt terrible about the whole thing. He was an unhappy young man. And of course I had just had a bout with the governor. I was angry with him, and what I had to say didn't make him feel any better."

"He believed in what he had done," I said.

Gott swiveled his eyes to me. "Yes, I'm sure he did."

"But his career was ruined," I said.

"No, no, I don't think so," Gott's voice was rumbly and

judicious. "He may have thought it was ruined, but. . ." He ducked
his head and looked at me from beneath his graying eyebrows. "I
liked Orson." He pointed at me. "You were at the funeral. You
remember that one speaker who said Orson wanted to be a rancher
when he was younger and he treated the public land like it was his
own?"

"LaVar Hafen," I said.

"Yes. Well, what he said was true. Orson cared. And he was
smart enough to keep track of the little details and at the same time
not lose sight of the big policy." Gott wiggled his fingers to show
little details and spread his arms to show the big policy. "You
know," he said, "I've spent thirty years in the Bureau. But I can still
remember when I was Orson's age, and I was frustrated and
impatient. I wanted to express myself, to make land policy the way
I thought it should be made." He moved his hands in front of him,
fingers wiggling. "It takes a lot of years to get where you can express
yourself in this business," Gott said. I glanced at his rough-hewn
desk and cow-horn chair. "Of course, I wouldn't want any of this
publicized," Gott said.

"Back on the record," I said. "Did Orson's death make it
possible to change the ruling on CalCom's coal?"

"We're a government agency, Al. We make decisions according to the rules. Orson's death was tragic, but it didn't affect any
decision we made in this office, and I don't know any reason anyone
would think otherwise."

"Jones threatened a $10 billion project," I said. "The governor
was so concerned he came here for the first time ever to lobby you,
and you made an extra effort to do what the governor wanted. You
transferred Jones to a non-job. Then Jones was murdered, and the
project is now back on track."

"Al, you're trying to make it sound as if there's some dark
conspiracy here. There's no conspiracy, Al, believe me. We're just

trying to make a timely decision here in the public interest, that's all."

"Can I have a copy of Jones's letter to CalCom?" I asked.

"What?" Gott ran his hand over his hair from left to right.

"It's a public document. Can I have a copy?"

"Well, of course this office believes in being open with the press, but that would be an internal working document, isn't that right, Jack?"

"You bet."

"It's not internal. It was sent to CalCom," I said.

"Yes, but it's part of our internal decision-making process," Gott said.

"No, you said it wasn't part of your decision-making loop."

Gott leaned his head back and looked at me through half-closed eyes. "Of course, you'd be welcome to the document, but we gave a copy to the police, didn't we, Jack?"

"Yes, sir, last week."

"Well, of course, we wouldn't want to interfere in any way with their ongoing investigation. You'll be welcome to a copy of that document as soon as they've concluded their investigation and the matter is resolved in court. That would be our media-relations policy in this case, wouldn't it, Jack?"

"You bet," Hampton's eyes remained locked on the open sky.

I looked at Gott. His face was blank. I could see he wasn't going to clarify any parameters for me on this issue within this timeframe. "Thanks for your help," I said.

"We're always happy to help the news media," Gott said.

"You bet," said Hampton.

twenty-six

**Investigation Slow
in Foothill Shooting**

Lieutenant Wilford Benton leaned back in the swivel chair behind his gray metal desk and stretched his arms upwards. "Al Cannon, reporter at la-ah-arge," he said behind a yawn. He was not expecting me to have startling information.

I was nonplussed. I had gotten in by telling Benton I had more information, but unlike the last time, what I had now wasn't very helpful. I started piecing together in my mind bits of speculation and facts of dubious relevance, which I hoped would sound helpful enough to land another *Telegram* exclusive. A yawn was not encouraging.

It was even more galling because in all justice I should not have been in Benton's office at all that morning. I should have been enjoying time off.

I had returned from Price after

two long days on the road and filed separate stories on Persevere, the proposed plant site, Nick Vassos, the BLM decision to let CalCom have Vassos's coal leases, and the interview with Merrill Gott. That was more than a week's work for any reporter.

But Barry Bowen makes a living on ingratitude. "What do you have for tomorrow, Al?" he had asked.

"I'm going to take tomorrow off, Barry."

"I thought you wanted this beat, Al. You don't want it, just say so." Bowen sounded as if he were honestly puzzled, all the better to deliver his punch line. "Mary Beth wants it. She damn near cried when I sent her back to the cop shop. I'll call her right now, if you want, and tell her she can have it back."

"I'll have to work Saturday, too," I said. "I've got that Blue Sky Coalition trip to Persevere."

Bowen looked uncomfortable. "Why don't you take Saturday off."

"No, it's a good story. I hear Lanny Barrington's going to come. I'll do it," I said in a public-spirited way.

Bowen said, "I thought I'd send Mary Beth on that. You know, some consolation for losing the beat."

"If you're going to give her the story anyway, I'll take a couple of days off," I said.

So here I was, trying to cozen a story out of Lieutenant Wilford Benton instead of enjoying a deserved rest. I had defeated Bowen's plan to reduce my standing at the *Telegram*, but I was not yet enjoying the fruits of victory. There is no reason to grow old in journalism if you can't fool the bosses and loaf when you want. In any case, there was nothing for it now but to try my line on Benton. "Have you talked to Rambeau?" I asked.

"We talked to him."

"He has a theory about Jones's killing."

Benton looked at me and said nothing, waiting for me to

continue, letting me know that he remembered I had promised him information on the telephone.

"He thinks Jones may have been killed because he was a threat to the CalCom power project."

Benton continued to look at me without saying anything. His eyelids drooped a little, as if he were getting sleepy.

"He says you've got to begin by asking who benefitted from Jones's death, and the answer is CalCom," I said.

"Does he have any evidence?" Benton asked.

"I asked him that. He said it's a theory, a hypothesis, a direction to investigate, not a proven case."

"We already got lotsa directions to investigate."

"Really?" I asked, trying to sieze the opening.

"We're not ready to release further information to the media at this time," Benton said. I could tell he suspected I was trying to bilk him for a story.

"Did Rambeau tell you his theory when you talked to him?' I asked.

"He mentioned it, but in police work we try to deal with facts."

"I didn't pay much attention either until yesterday when the BLM gave those coal leases back to CalCom."

"Yeah, I saw that in the paper."

"Rambeau predicted CalCom would get that coal after Jones was dead."

"Just because CalCom got some coal doesn't mean they killed somebody," Benton said.

"A theory becomes more believable when it generates true predictions," I said.

Benton looked away from me, obviously uninterested in verification theory and other points in the philosophy of knowledge. "The problem I got with that theory is this," he said. "Maybe it helped CalCom for Jones to die. I mean they claim they bought more coal and everything, so they really didn't need for Jones to be overruled. But let's say Jones's death helped them the way Rambeau says it did."

He paused and looked at me to see if I accepted his premise. I nodded. "This is all off the record," he said. "I don't want to read where I'm speculating about some citizen being involved in a homicide-type situation."

I nodded.

"Okay, say they were helped. Still it's the company gets the help. I mean Bywater, Kilee, all those guys, they may want this project, but they draw a paycheck whether they get it or not, right?"

I nodded.

"So they gonna murder someone, help the company? You gotta be a pretty loyal employee to do something like that." Benton looked at me hard again, "Off the record," he said.

I nodded.

He said, "I'll start taking the 'who benefits' stuff seriously when I see someone get personal benefit. Like the murder helps them personally. I don't know anyone now it helps personally."

I said, "Rambeau says the Utah establishment is reluctant to investigate CalCom because they want the project so badly."

"Some guys always blame the establishment."

"Well, the governor did call Hastings at the *Telegram* to try to kill stories about the project. And Hastings in fact killed a story about Rambeau's theories," I said.

"Yeah? Killed your story?" An inward half-smile, such as might have been painted by Da Vinci, flicked across Benton's craggy face. "I heard you got in trouble over there." The idea that I might have difficulty at the *Telegram* seemed to please Benton.

"No, it wasn't my story. It was Mary Beth Kearney's."

"Mm," he frowned slightly. "That's why she's back here at the cop shop?"

He took no pleasure in trouble for Kearney. Indeed, he seemed to take a fatherly interest in her. I wondered if she called him Wilf-babes.

"The *governor* got her put back here?" Benton couldn't believe that was true.

"No, not directly. Bywater was the one who complained about that story. But Hastings is especially sensitive about the whole issue because he knows the governor is interested." I was glad to mention the governor, Bywater, and Hastings. Maybe I could impress Benton with my own establishment credentials.

Benton leaned back in his swivel chair until it touched the gray metal filing cabinet behind him, the one with the gold bowling trophy on top. "Actually, we've expended considerable investigative resources on the victim's employment at the BLM and on the CalCom Project looking for a motive for the attack. So far we haven't found much."

"Have you found much anywhere else?" I asked.

"Not really," Benton said.

"Gott told me you have a copy of the letter Jones sent to CalCom," I said. "The one that said their coal leases may be invalid."

"Yeah, after you told us about it we got a copy for the file."

I was glad he remembered I had told him about it. "Could I have a copy?" I asked in my most polite voice.

"Our investigative files aren't available to non-law-enforcement personnel," Benton said. He was making needless difficulties. I supposed he didn't want to encourage reporters trying to cadge a story from him without bringing any information.

Later, back at the *Telegram,* Barry Bowen said, "This isn't much of a story, Al."

"Best I could do," I shrugged.

"If we're going to give you the beat, Al, we expect some enterprise."

Bowen had about used up the threat of taking me off the

CalCom story. "Sometimes you eat the bear," I said, "and sometimes the bear eats you." I turned away from him back to my word processor.

twenty-seven

"Project Would Heat the World," Coalition Says

by Al Cannon

The Blue Sky Coalition bus stood in the parking lot behind the State Capitol Saturday before dawn. The motor thrummed softly and blew warm air from vents on its rear flank. The driver saw me coming and swung the door open before I could knock. Inside, the bus was light and cozy after the chilly dark of the parking lot. About half the seats were filled with reporters, photographers, and environmentalists.

"Is Mary Beth coming?" Paul Rambeau asked. He was sitting in the front seat opposite the driver with a clipboard in his lap, checking off names as people arrived.

"No, they sent me, instead. She's covering the police beat now."

"Oh." His disappointment showed.

"Is Lanny Barrington coming?" I asked.

"She'll meet us," he said. "NBC is coming, too. They've sent a crew from Los Angeles. They're taking their own transportation."

As I walked past him down the aisle he added, "*People Magazine* is coming, too."

I recognized half-a-dozen reporters from press and television. Two TV photographers were stowing gear in empty seats and overhead racks. Most of the passengers were environmentalists rallying against the CalCom Project. I found a double seat for myself near the middle of the bus. Jane Belkirk of Channel 5 and her photographer straggled in five minutes late. Jane carried the big wooden tripod for the camera over her shoulder; people ducked as she walked down the aisle.

As soon as Channel 5 was settled, Rambeau stood up and said, "Welcome to the Blue-Sky CalCom-Busting Tour Bus." Members of the Blue Sky Coalition cheered, clapped, and whistled. "We'll be going down to Lost Sheep Lookout near the site where our revered governor, Parley Smith Wells, in his wisdom, and his concern for Utah, a pretty great state, has decided to put the largest coal-fired power plant ever built in America." Members of the Blue Sky Coalition booed and laughed. From the back of the bus someone shouted "No way, Par-lay," giving a hillbilly twang to the governor's name.

Rambeau held up his hand. "We will be joined in Green River by Lanny Barrington. She'll come with us to Lost Sheep Lookout. There we'll be able to see the proposed site of the plant, and Ms. Barrington will point out some facts about the plant and how it would destroy the unique and fragile beauty of that area."

"No way, Par-lay," the man in the back yelled again. I turned to look. He was a young man in a maroon beret, black-rimmed glasses, and a black nylon windbreaker. Paul Rambeau sat down, and the bus headed for the freeway and the long ride to southern Utah.

I bunched my jacket up against the side of the bus to use as a pillow for a couple of hours' sleep. But a robust young woman in her early twenties plopped down in the seat next to me and said, "Hi, I'm Jenny Lingford. Could I show you some of the information we have?" She had short dark hair, large dark eyes, and round tan cheeks. She wore a persimmon-colored pullover with large, black zippers at the throat and side pockets, and a black "Patagonia" label on the chest.

"Look at these numbers," she said, and handed me a sheet worked up on somebody's personal computer. "These are really incredible." Across the aisle, a skinny young man with a lilac-colored bandana tied over his blonde hair was handing a copy of the same sheet to the *Deseret News* reporter. The Blue Sky Coalition planned to use the long bus ride to present its case to the press.

"Thanks," I said, folded up the sheet of paper, and put it in my shirt pocket. I intended be polite but unresponsive in hopes that Jenny Lingford would go away, or talk to someone else, or run out of things to say, and I could go to sleep.

"Look at this," she said pointing to a line in a table of figures on the copy of the paper she kept. "I don't know why we never see this in the newspaper. I mean, this plant will put out thousands of tons of nitrogen oxides every day. I mean, it'll turn the sky brown all the way to Grand Canyon."

"Mmm."

"And you've heard them talking about scrubbers?" She held the sheet next to her chest, so she could show me her number as a surprise.

"Mm-hmm."

"Well look at how much sulfur will get past their so-called control technology. Look at that! It'll all come down as acid rain in the East." Lingford opened the palm of her hand and shook it in frustration at the inability of people to see what was as open and obvious as her palm. "And then they wonder why they've got 128 dead lakes in the Catskills."

I retrieved the paper she had given me from my shirt pocket and began to study the numbers, resigned to no more sleep. "Where'd you learn about this?" I asked.

"I studied it," she said. "I'm a nursing student, but stopping this plant is more important for human health." She returned to her theme. "CalCom just lies about pollution. I mean, they don't even include carbon dioxide in their emissions figures. But that's the most important greenhouse gas. I mean, it's just totally screwing up the whole world's weather, that's all."

Lingford explained in detail the dangers of global warming from the greenhouse effect and how CalCom would hasten the world toward climatological disaster. I yawned and said I could get the numbers off the sheet she had so kindly provided. But she remained patient and didn't skip a single statistic.

Across the aisle, the skinny man with the lilac-colored bandana had finished his lecture and was telling stories. The stories sounded interesting. In the seat in front of him the *Deseret News* photographer was turned around, kneeling in his seat with his elbows resting on the seatback to listen. Rambeau had wandered back from the front of the bus and was resting one buttock on the armrest of a seat to hear the story-teller.

I shifted in my seat and looked past Lingford, hoping to direct her attention to the stories. She followed my gaze and said, "That's Bill Tucker." Then to my relief, she turned and listened. Though I wanted sleep, I listened, too. Indeed, I did my best to appear fascinated. Evidently Lingford considered outdoor stories sufficiently edifying, but I feared she might find sleep a neglect of my responsibilities and call me back to my duty by resuming her lecture on emission gasses.

"I remember, I didn't want them to find my body," Tucker was saying. "I didn't want some podunk jeep-rescue team hauling me out in a rubber body-bag and complaining about how I stunk." He smiled, amused now by the way his mind had worked when he had been lost in the desert and might have died of thirst. "I was looking for a hole in the rock I could crawl into and die, and only the vultures and worms would ever find me."

The *Deseret News* reporter said, "They would have had to look for you for two weeks. It would have driven them crazy." He grinned at the idea of a joke played on a rural jeep rescue team.

"'We just cain't find that boy. He musta found himself a hole somewheres,'" Tucker said, imitating one of the imaginary searchers. His accent sounded like that of a rural redneck rather than of a southern Utahn.

Tucker wore a gold stud in his left earlobe and a faded white sweatshirt with the picture of a freight train and the words "Stop the Cancer Cannonball" stenciled on the front, a souvenir from a past environmental battle. He spread his hands histrionically and quoted from memory: "To die in the open, under the sky, far from the insolent interference of leech and priest, that surely would be a stroke of rare good fortune," and his handsome smile broadened into a grin.

As the story turned out though, Tucker was denied that particular piece of rare good fortune. He found water. Not quickly. He recounted his parched wanderings alone across the slick rock and red sands, beneath the relentless sun. If he hadn't found the hole in the rock holding a puddle of scummy water when he did, he would soon have lain down and given up. "It was full of mosquito larvae and deer turds, but it was the best water I ever tasted," he said.

The bus took the same familiar route south, but when it reached I-70 it turned off to Green River. Rambeau explained that Persevere didn't have an airport and Green River had the closest air strip for Lanny Barrington flying in from California. The bus parked in front of Green River Drug on the wide main street.

A white Chevy Blazer waited across the street. It made a U turn and pulled up in front of the bus. "That's NBC," Rambeau said. He hurried from the bus to talk to the crew. Through the bus window, I saw him shake hands with the correspondent, John Markston. Markston is about as old as I am, and about as stout. He wore a pressed, khaki shirt, and a neatly trimmed graying beard.

The NBC photographer got out, pulled down the tailgate, and took out his camera. He pointed the camera at the fender of the Blazer to white-balance in the midday sun, then set the camera on the ground between his feet and leaned against the side of the truck. He was in his thirties and was the only black person I'd seen all day.

When the Salt Lake photographers saw NBC gearing up, they picked up their cameras and got off the bus in case something interesting was about to happen. The rest of the passengers followed them and milled around on the sidewalk. The environmentalists stretched and laughed in the autumn sunshine. They were young, lithe, and healthy, happy to be on an outing where they would make national news, and save pristine air from defilement by corporate America.

Diesel trucks drove through Green River, stopping at service stations and cafes and leaving clouds of exhaust that roiled and danced in the sunlight. Two girls about ten rode double on a bicycle along the sidewalk. They dismounted and pushed the bicycle to the edge of the small crowd. A man in bib overalls and a pink bill cap with "Reebok" on the front strolled along the sidewalk with his overweight wife. They stopped to look.

The young girl pushing the bicycle recognized Jane Belkirk, from Channel 5. "You're on TV, aren't you?" she said.

Jane Belkirk smiled and said, "Yes, what's your name?"

"Melinda," the girl said, and smiled shyly. Two teenaged boys in a faded red pickup truck sped past and tooted their horn at the crowd. From inside the drugstore two elderly women eyed us through the plate-glass window.

"Is Barrington coming?" Markston asked Rambeau.

"Yeah, she's flying in, supposed to be here pretty soon," Rambeau said, looking at his watch.

"Do you know when?" Markston asked. He was anxious. If Barrington didn't come, he wouldn't have a story.

The man wearing bib overalls and the pink Reebok cap stood with his wife looking at the crowd and the TV cameras. "What's news?" he asked the Channel 2 photographer.

"It's the Blue Sky Coalition tour here to see the site for the CalCom plant," the photographer said.

"You going out to the project?" the man asked.

"I think so," the photographer said.

"Well, we need that project. We got to have some natural resource activity down in this area," the man in bib overalls said. The photographer didn't say anything.

"You environmentalists?" the man asked.

"I'm just the photographer." The photographer didn't face the man squarely. He stood with his hands in his Levi pockets, looking down the street.

"Well, we sure hope you aren't down here to obstruct the project." The man's wife put her hand on his arm.

John Markston had been standing with his arms folded, shuffling his feet, and peering down the street for Lanny Barrington. He turned and looked at the man in bib overalls.

"What's your name, sir?"

"Hyrum Shumway."

"Could I interview you on camera?"

"What about?"

"About what you were just saying."

"You bet." Shumway grinned to show he was pleased and friendly, and didn't take being on TV too seriously. Markston looked over his shoulder at his photographer, who had already picked up the camera and was walking over to where Markston and Shumway stood. The NBC sound man got a black graphite tripod out of the back of the Blazer and set it up by the photographer. Mrs. Shumway backed well away so she wouldn't be in the picture.

"What station'll this be on?" Shumway asked.

"I'm with NBC, and this'll be on the *Today Show* tomorrow, I think, if Lanny Barrington shows up."

"Lanny Barrington coming here?"

"I hope so."

"The one in the movies?"

Markston nodded. The photographer fixed the camera on top of the tripod and adjusted the length of the legs so the camera was level at the height of Shumway's face. Markston said, "Take your hat off, would you please, Hyrum? It makes a shadow across your face."

"You're gonna have me squinting in the sun," Shumway said. But he took off the cap and held it by his side. He was bald on top, gray around the sides. Sun and wind had affected his face about the way they affected the country. Gullies ran down his forehead. The long hairs of his eyebrows twisted out at various untamed angles like a stand of cedars on an exposed ridge. Odd shapes were sculpted in low relief on his red cheeks.

"Yeah, that's better," the photographer said. People formed a loose arc behind Markston and the camera to listen to the interview.

"How do people here feel about the California Commonwealth Utah Project, Mr. Shumway?" Markston asked.

"We gotta have it. No question about that. We're pretty depressed here, anymore. We need some economic development."

"Would the plant ruin the environment?"

"No. No it won't. Won't do any harm at all, hardly."

Rambeau said, "Here they come." A blue Bronco with a silver stripe on the side came down the street and parked behind the bus.

Markston turned his head to look, but Shumway kept right on talking. "We had industrial factories here before, during the uranium boom and everything. I don't think they was as big as this one, but they didn't wreck the environment. Once this one's in, I don't think you'll even notice it's there, hardly."

Except for Markston and his camera crew, the crowd had turned to see Lanny Barrington. She stepped out the passenger door of the Bronco, smiled, leaned her head back, and ran her fingers through her short, blonde hair. Two men got out of the back seat, one of them carrying a still camera. "That's the *People Magazine* reporter," Rambeau said.

Barrington said, "Isn't it a fantastic day?" She wore a light-blue workshirt and snug-fitting Levis, and she carried a gray nylon bag with a strap over her shoulder.

Rambeau stepped forward. "I'm Paul Rambeau, we met once at a fundraiser at Bob's."

"Of course, Paul, I remember." She hugged Rambeau. Then she surveyed the members of the Blue Sky Coalition and the television cameras, "I'm proud to be here. You're on the front lines. You're the reason —"

"I don't really understand what all the fuss's about, myself." Shumway was still talking to the NBC camera. "People build power plants all the time. We need this one here to help us out. It's a real opportunity for us."

Barrington looked past the TV cameras pointed at her and through the ragged crowd to see who was interrupting her entrance. Then she walked over and stood by Markston's camera to watch the interview. "Does it make you mad?" Markston was asking Shumway.

Shumway recognized Barrington and glanced at her nervously. "Well, it doesn't make me happy. We kinda think we're the ones that live here, and we ought to have some say in what goes on. But we don't, not hardly. The BLMers control all the land, and now these environmentalists coming in from all over the country, telling us how to do things here."

"But this land is a treasure for all Americans," Barrington said in the thrilling voice she used for the message lines in her critically acclaimed films showing the pluck of a mother deserted by her husband, or the resourcefulness of a reporter exposing a corrupt and murderous police department. "This may be America's last chance to save a remnant of clean air and natural beauty as a place to renew our spirits."

As Barrington spoke, she stepped forward in front of the NBC camera. Markston stepped out of the way and looked at his cameraman to make sure the conversation between Barrington and Shumway was being photographed. The experienced cameraman kept his eye to the viewfinder. All the other photographers turned their cameras and began shooting the conversation, too.

As Barrington stepped forward, Shumway stepped back. He hadn't planned on getting into a televised argument with a movie star. "Well, we're sure glad to have you people come here to renew your spirits, or whatever. But we got to make a living, too."

"I know, I know, the big corporations tell us we've got to let them rape the whole country or we'll all be poor. But that isn't true. We don't need more electricity or more smog or more people. And we won't let the corporations take over this wonderful land just for their own selfish profit." A few members of the Blue Sky Coalition clapped.

"Well, I suppose they gotta make a profit to stay in business same as everybody else," Shumway said.

"But some things aren't for sale," said Barrington, "and this absolutely stunning country should be one of them." More of the crowd clapped and said "yeah" or "that's right."

"I guess it may not be for sale if you're rich, but we got to have some jobs and economic development here."

Jane Belkirk was standing behind Shumway. She asked, "What about global warming?" Markston gave her a disgusted look. A spontaneous confrontation between Barrington and a local man was perfect for network television, and he was nettled that a bush-league local reporter couldn't stay quiet and let the good material happen.

Shumway looked around at the crowd, not sure where the question came from. "I don't think it's getting any warmer. It was real cold here last winter."

Members of the crowd laughed. "You don't know what you're talking about," the young man in the maroon beret and black nylon windbreaker said.

Jenny Lingford spoke up. "Global warming is a threat to the whole earth. There's more at stake here than a few jobs. There really is."

Shumway looked at Lingford with his mouth open and his brow furrowed. "Well, young lady, if you're concerned about the whole earth, why'd you all come here? You make a lot more pollution in Salt Lake or Los Angeles. Why don't you clean up first where you come from?"

A number of environmentalists spoke at once, and the circle of people tightened around Shumway. Belkirk from Channel 5 had the most penetrating voice. "Does it make people here angry? Will they become violent?"

Shumway faced Belkirk and shook his head. "No. We're not violent. It's the environmentalists who've been violent, killing cattle and gumming up construction equipment."

"What about the death threats?" Lingford asked. Shumway turned to answer her but was distracted by Bill Tucker who had almost died on the desert. "You don't have any proof. You shouldn't be saying that," he shouted.

"Well, I think it's clear radical environmentalists killed those cattle over Emery County and the ones down by Boulder, too. I'm not saying any of you did . . ."

The young man in the maroon beret shouted, "That's an irresponsible accusation."

Lingford leaned over and stuck her face close in front of Shumway's. "What about the death threats?" she asked.

"What death threats?"

"Someone called the Blue Sky Coalition Headquarters and said they'd shoot environmentalists who came down here."

"What makes you think it was any of us?"

"What makes you think it was any of us killed the cattle?" the young man in the maroon beret shouted back.

Barrington put one hand on Shumway's forearm and raised her other to quiet the crowd. "We are really on your side," she said to Shumway, "and we come as friends."

Shumway looked at Barrington with relief. "Well, you're sure welcome here. We don't get to see many famous people like you," he said. He grasped the hand she had placed on his forearm and shook it vigorously.

Rambeau said, "Lanny's on a real tight schedule. We need to get moving." He began herding people back onto the bus.

I slipped past Rambeau and ran into the drugstore to phone a story into the paper. I used the numbers on the sheet that Lingford had given me and didn't mention Barrington, saving her for a new story tomorrow.

Rambeau got a little grumpy when I was the last one back on the bus. But my story was the only one to make the Saturday papers, so it was worth it.

twenty-eight

"**Stop the Greed Machine,**" **Says Star**

by Al Cannon

As the bus drove to Lost Sheep Lookout, Lanny Barrington walked down the aisle shaking hands. The *People Magazine* photographer backed down the aisle ahead of her, camera to his face, flash popping. Rambeau and the *People* reporter followed her.

"Thank you for coming all this way to help us out," Jenny Lingford said as she shook hands.

"No, thank *you*," Barrington said. "It's thanks to people like you that we have a chance to stop this thing." She leaned against the seat in front of Lingford to brace herself against the roll of the moving bus and extended her hand to me. "Oh, don't get up," she said. "Buses really aren't made for introductions."

There were wrinkles around her eyes, and faint smile-shaped lines at the corners of her mouth. Barrington no longer plays daring sex-kitten roles, but she still lands romantic female leads. Close to her, I could tell her allure in film now comes as much from her art as from her beauty, and I thought more highly of her power as an actress after seeing her face plain. She whispered to Rambeau, "When I've said hello to these nice people, I'll need a little time to go over my notes."

After a few more handshakes, Barrington returned to the front of the bus. She took a notebook out of her gray nylon bag and silently moved her lips as she rehearsed what she would say. Rambeau walked back and stood in the aisle by the *People* reporter, who had slipped into a seat behind Bill Tucker. "That's why we're not going to Persevere," Rambeau said. "We'd get lynched there. That was enough confrontation, just in Green River."

"It was rather good for pictures, though," *People* said. He was a smooth and pale young man, with light-brown hair that swept back from his forehead in a glistening sheen of peaks and waves. His long-sleeved, green corduroy shirt was buttoned clear up to his neck.

"Yeah, wasn't she great?" Rambeau said. "I mean, she got the action going back there with that farmer, and then she cut it off, at just the right moment, so it wouldn't seem like the guy was being picked on or anything. She really knows how to handle cameras."

"How did you ever get her to come?" *People* asked. He spoke with what might have been a slight English accent. But I don't think he was English. I think he chose that as the way he wanted to talk.

"She's a real environmentalist. I mean she's studied this issue. She isn't here just to get headlines," Rambeau said. "And I asked her because I thought maybe you guys would come."

"Yes," *People* agreed, "I'm afraid we wouldn't be interested in a story about a power plant alone." He raised his eyebrows and cocked his head judiciously. "Lanny makes it rather a good story, actually. It might even make cover."

"Really, the cover?"

"Maybe. Of course, you never know what they'll pick. But saving the earth is very important."

Rambeau grabbed hold of the luggage rack to steady himself in the swaying bus and looked at the *People* reporter. "I think a cover story on this issue now would be decisive. It would show the bureaucrats and congressmen in Washington that it isn't just tree-huggers who care about this issue. A cover story could turn the whole movement around."

People thought for a few seconds about what Rambeau said. Then he wrinkled his nose. "That was a very ugly little town. I suppose they're as poor as that man said they are."

Rambeau nodded. "People here have outstripped the land's carrying capacity."

"They breed like rabbits in southern Utah," Jenny Lingford said. "They have like ten kids a family."

"There's no way the land can support all the people," Rambeau said.

"Unless they get the plant," I said.

Rambeau looked at me. "They can increase the population here for a little while, a few decades, by destroying the environment and by damaging the earth's atmosphere. But we won't let them do that."

People Magazine turned slightly in his seat, and looked up at Rambeau. "Is it true what that man said, that environmentalists shoot cattle?"

Rambeau shook his head. "We obey the law."

Tucker leaned forward in his aisle seat behind *People.* "There's no evidence environmentalists killed any cattle. But whoever it was did a real good thing."

Rambeau said, "You know, pretty soon the whole world will be overloaded like southern Utah." He wanted to deflect the conversation away from cattle.

Tucker was not deflected. "Everywhere you go there are those damn cows, and they crap all over everything. You know, they crap methane, and that's the worst greenhouse gas there is. And the government gives ranchers this really outrageous sweetheart deal so they hardly pay anything for grazing on public land and the cattle overgraze and bring desertification. And the only reason for it is so people can eat dead cows and give themselves heart attacks." Tucker put his hand on his chest. "I don't believe in shooting anything, myself. But if you have to shoot something, a cow's probably the best thing."

Lingford said, "There's only been one or two incidents of cattle shooting. That's nothing compared to what CalCom's done. They murdered a government official in Salt Lake."

"Oh? I hadn't heard about that. Have there been charges?" *People* asked. He looked at Lingford and blinked his eyes several times.

Rambeau said, "No charges. But they're the ones who benefitted from the murder." For the next two minutes Rambeau explained how Orson Jones had stopped CalCom from getting coal leases, and then how CalCom got the coal back after Jones was murdered.

Lingford said, "Orson Jones was the only one who had the courage to stop the project, and they killed him." She set her mouth in anger and looked as if she might cry.

"Yes, well that does sound very serious," *People* said. He had a leather-covered notebook and a silver pen, and he began taking notes.

Rambeau said, "Al here wrote about the shooting. Even the Salt Lake cops could see it was a pre-meditated murder. I mean, the killer hid in wait and everything." He turned around and looked at me for confirmation. I nodded.

"Haven't the police done anything?" *People* asked. He was still writing.

"Not much," Rambeau said. He grabbed the luggage rack again as the bus lurched. "You can't believe how much the Utah establishment wants this project. All they can see in this whole thing is jobs and money. And all they care about's money. The last thing they want is for some investigation that would expose the ugly underside of this whole deal."

"And they haven't done anything about the death threats, either," Lingford said.

"Oh? Death threats?"

"Some rednecks down here called the Blue Sky Coalition offices with anonymous death threats," she said.

"The office in Salt Lake?"

"Yes."

"How do you know it was people from around here?" *People* asked. Lingford thought about the question for a second and looked to Rambeau for help.

"Well, we don't, really," Rambeau said. "But it sounded like it from the accent, you know: 'You people come down here making trouble and your lives aren't safe.' Like that."

"Did you take the call?" *People* asked.

"Yeah, you know, it makes you admire Lanny even more. I mean, I was up-front with her about the phone call and everything, but she still just came right out to Utah. You can understand now why I didn't want to go to Persevere."

"NBC's going to Persevere, aren't they. Did you warn them?" *People* asked.

"No, I haven't," Rambeau said. He looked out the window at the NBC Blazer following the bus. "Maybe I should." Rambeau and *People* talked more about Jones's murder and the threatening phone call. I started thinking about the murder and stopped listening to what they said.

The bus turned off the pavement onto a dirt road, and Rambeau leaned over to look out the window again and make sure NBC made the turnoff. The road climbed in switchbacks up the side of a mesa, and then bumped along the top between twisted cedar trees and runty sagebrush that grew sparsely on the stony red soil. After four or five miles the unpaved road ended in a wide space of red dirt that served as a parking lot.

"Everybody out," Rambeau yelled. Photographers gathered up their gear, and people followed Rambeau out of the bus. "It's over there," Rambeau pointed, and we trudged a couple of hundred yards to the edge of the plateau.

The edge was sandstone, grainy, maroon, and crumbling from the buffetings of rain and frost. The side was steep, but it looked as if you could climb down using your hands. A few bunches of brown grass and gnarled junipers grew out of cracks in the rock, working patiently to rip it apart. At the bottom, maybe 800 feet below, the land undulated away in patterns of dry washes and low hills spotted with rock formations. Wind and water had shaped the stone into towers, humps, fins and ridges. Some layers of the exposed rocks were white, like the sandy beaches of an ancient, shallow sea. Most of the rocks were shades of red, ranging from pink to maroon, where rusted iron colored the sand. In the middle distance stood several other plateaus about as high as the one we were on, and beyond them were blue-green mountains.

"Let's do it here," the NBC photographer said, pointing to a slight depression in the edge of the plateau. "We'll shoot down a little, and that way we'll be able to see the view behind her." Lanny Barrington walked to where the photographer pointed.

Rambeau objected. "If you shoot that way, you won't be able to get the plant site in the background. It's on that plateau over there," he said pointing. "If they build it, you'll be able to see it from here big as life, right there, spoiling the whole view. That's why we came here, so we could see the plant site."

The photographer looked at the distant plateau and shook his head. "Won't be able to tell one buncha red rocks from another behind her on TV. This'll be the shot." Photographers set their TV cameras close together in line ten feet from where Barrington stood.

She turned her back to the crowd to slide microphone wires under her shirt at the beltline, and clip the small black microphones to her collar.

"Ready?" she asked when she turned around.

The NBC photographer looked down the line of cameras at the other photographers and said, "Yeah."

Barrington looked down, then back up again, "What is at stake here is the health of the earth," she said. "The earth is the mother of us all. She is old, and as we can see here she is incredibly beautiful." Barrington was able to talk so the forty people standing behind the cameras could hear and still sound as if she were conversing instead of orating.

"Americans are making the earth sick," she said. "We are becoming a greed machine. We destroy what is good, and natural, and beautiful." She raised her voice. "Friends, here is where we stop the American greed machine." Environmentalists clapped and cheered. Television cameras swiveled on their tripods to catch the crowd's enthusiasm. Barrington stood with her left hand stretched out, palm upward over the wide view. She gazed over the tops of the crowd and cameras as if seeing a bright environmental future.

"You are fighting for a cause of transcendent moral urgency. If this monstrosity is built here in this beautiful desert where the greed machine hasn't reached, the message will go out that the people can't stop the corporations, and the greed machine will continue to poison the earth and sully the air."

It occurred to me then that I knew who had killed Orson Jones.

Barrington talked of conservation and of care for the earth and the air. I thought about the murder: Orson Jones was killed because of a conspiracy that included a speculator, a banker, and a government official. I could see how they profited from the scheme, and how the public events in this story followed the course of the hidden conspiracy like a line of willows follows a buried river through the desert.

"I salute you all for being here to fight for the future of the planet," Barrington said. Environmentalists cheered. Barrington said she would answer questions, and reporters asked about the effect of the plant on national parks and how she got personally involved in the environmental movement.

After ten minutes Barrington looked at her watch. Rambeau stepped forward into the space between Barrington and the crowd and said, "We promised Lanny we'd get her back so she could take off before dark, and we'll have to move quickly to keep that promise." There was a final round of ragged clapping.

John Markston asked if Barrington would walk along the rim and point to the plant site, which she did, while the cameras took pictures. Then she, Rambeau, and a couple of other environmentalists talked about the plant and how it would ruin the view, while the cameras took pictures of them standing on the edge and gesturing over miles of desolate countryside. Reporters interviewed Rambeau briefly. "I'll talk to you in the bus," he said. "We really have to get going."

I was thinking about explaining what I knew to Lieutenant Benton. Then I thought of a plan to goad the conspirators into acting, without letting them know that I understood what they had done. I walked over to Markston. "I hear you're going to Persevere," I said.

"Yeah, we've got to talk to some people on the other side."

"Could I bum a ride?" He hesitated, obviously not wanting another passenger. I said, "I know the mayor there. He says the town may die without the plant. He'd like to talk to you." Markston nodded.

I told Rambeau I would be riding to Persevere with NBC. We waited a few minutes while the photographer and sound man wound up the microphone wires and packed the camera and tripod in their white Blazer, then we hurried to get onto the narrow road off the mesa before the bus so we wouldn't have to follow in its dust.

twenty-nine

Gov. Lauds Rural Banker

It was almost sundown when we reached Persevere. Mayor Hafen was minding his store. "I don't think we've ever had a national TV personality come to Persevere before," he said grinning and pumping John Markston's hand. "We're real appreciative you gentlemen came all this way to get our side of the story."

The mayor shook hands with the photographer and sound man, too. They were going to set up lights and interview him in the store, but then Heber Hanson drove in to get gas. The photographer took pictures of the mayor helping Hanson pump gas, and then of Hanson and the mayor talking about deer hunting. So Markston decided to interview both Hanson and the mayor in front of the gas pumps.

I asked the mayor if I could use his phone. I was worried that Rulon

Crowe might not be in town. But he was. And after I told him what I wanted to talk about, he agreed to meet me at the bank. I walked the few blocks in the cool evening with a breeze blowing off the mountains and the pink light catching the willow trees in front of the red adobe houses on Main Street.

Crowe was standing by a blue Ford Bronco under the sign carved in flagstone that said "Bank Of Persevere." He didn't smile when we shook hands. It was the first time I had seen him without a coat and tie. He wore a blue-plaid, short-sleeved shirt, faded-blue denim pants, and gray jogging shoes. The outfit showed his thin shoulders and paunch. He still reminded me of DeGaulle.

"Let's go into the office," he said. He had a large bunch of keys in his hand. It took three to open the bank, two for the door and another for the alarm. We went through a lobby with two teller cages. They were old-fashioned with brass bars and marble stones to count money on. Behind them was the round steel door of the vault.

Crowe used another key to get into his office in the back. The office had old dormer windows with bars, and a large desk with pictures of Crowe and his family. He switched on the light, sat behind the desk, and motioned me to a high-backed, overstuffed chair.

"Now what did you say about the examiners?" he asked.

"I heard that the state bank examiners were coming here to look into irregularities in some loans."

"Our books are in order."

"What I heard was that there was no problem now, but you may have made some big loans with inadequate security in the recent past."

"Where did you hear this?" he asked. He sat straight in his padded swivel chair, and he squinted at me as if he were nearsighted and I were just a blur in his office.

"I promised I wouldn't tell. I understand I'm not supposed to know where the bank examiners are going before they get there. I just thought I'd do a story and wanted to ask you for a comment."

"I'm afraid I can't help you, Mr. Cannon. We don't discuss the bank's business, except I can assure you that our financial condition is sound and our books are in order."

"What I heard was you loaned money on coal leases to a speculator. I think maybe he eventually sold his interest to Cal-Com."

"I don't know who your source is, Mr. Cannon, but he seems to have told you a very detailed story," he said. A long, straight furrow appeared in his forehead above his long, straight nose.

"Did you make a loan that used coal leases as collateral?" I asked, and before he could answer I corrected myself. "Actually, what I heard was they weren't coal leases, they were options to buy coal leases. Highly speculative."

"As I said, we don't discuss the bank's business with the news media," Crowe said. "I really can't help you." He started to get out of his chair, to indicate the interview was over.

"There's more," I said. He stayed standing by his chair.

"The loan went sour, for a little while, at least. But, as you say, it was paid off in the end." I adjusted my glasses. "I guess normally no one would worry about a loan that turned out all right in the end. But what I heard is that with the savings and loan scandal, and all the national fuss, they thought they'd come and look at it."

"I didn't say anything about any loan, Mr. Cannon. I hope you don't misquote me. We don't discuss bank business."

"One other thing," I said. "I can't tell you who told me all this, but I wanted to warn you."

"Well, you've done that, and I appreciate it." He started to move around the desk.

"No, I haven't yet," I said. "I can't tell you who told me, but I can tell you that I've just been with a bunch of environmentalists over at Lost Sheep Lookout. I get the impression—just an impression—that this may be part of a plan to make trouble for you over the CalCom project, and they'll be using the S&L business as an excuse to push this thing harder than they normally would."

"That would be very inappropriate," he said. He took a step to his chair and sat back down. "If bank examiners are letting themselves be used to further the environmentalist agenda, then that undermines the integrity of the bank examination process." His gray eyes focussed on me through his bifocals. "Harassment of that kind would be unacceptable."

"Well, I could be wrong," I said.

Crowe gestured towards three photographs in glass-covered frames on the wall of his office to my right. "Let me just tell you, this bank has been in business seventy-four years. I'm the third generation Crowe to run this bank in Persevere."

The first photograph showed a skinny man in a wing collar, black suit, and felt hat standing in a dirt road in front of the Bank of Persevere. The second photo showed a man in a double breasted suit standing in the bank lobby in front of one of the teller cages with brass bars I had seen on the way in. The third was a color studio-portrait of Crowe. All three looked equally solemn.

"You don't find many small, family lenders like this one left. Most of them have sold out to First Security or Zions." He held up a hand. "Now those are good banks. And they do a professional job. They wanted to acquire this bank, too. But we wouldn't sell. No matter how professional a First Security or a Zions is, they don't care about Persevere the way we care about Persevere. This bank operates in the community interest, Mr. Cannon."

I nodded, glad that I had him talking.

"We make prudent loans. We wouldn't have survived this difficult regional economy if we weren't cautious. But the free enterprise system requires risk, and we do take careful risks that benefit our community."

I nodded again, but I may have looked skeptical.

"Let me share something with you, Mr. Cannon." He opened his desk drawer, searched briefly, and handed me a letter. "From the Office of Governor Parley Smith Wells" was the letterhead. "Dear Rulon," the letter said. "As you know, my administration has been dedicated to economic development in Utah." The first paragraph went on at some length detailing several "creative initiatives undertaken pro-actively" by the Wells administration.

Then in a shorter paragraph the governor wrote, "No one is in a more advantageous position to help Utah's economic development than its bankers. I am aware of the cooperation you have shown and the risks you have taken to further the great California Commonwealth Electric Power Project in your part of the state. Let me take this opportunity to commend you as a banker dedicated to his community and to the goal we all share of a prosperous and growing Utah." The letter was signed, "Parley Smith Wells, Governor." I took out my reporters' notebook and wrote down phrases from the letter.

"I really think it would be better if we didn't put anything about this in the paper," Crowe said.

"I'll just do a story about the letter and about how you've survived down here for seventy-four years and have helped the community. I won't mention the bank examiners and the environmentalists," I said, continuing to take notes.

"Oh, I suppose that might be all right," Crowe said. "In fact, I think that could be a positive development."

I got up and shook Crowe's hand. "Good luck," I said.

"I appreciate the professional way you've handled this," he said. We left the empty bank in mutual good feeling. I figured he'd taken the hook.

thirty

As it turned out, I had made a small miscalculation. I succeeded in provoking action from the conspirators as I intended, but I failed to anticipate the timing and direction of their counterstroke. Monday morning I came in to the *Telegram* late—fully justified, of course, because I had worked a long day on Saturday, stayed over at the Red Rock Motel in Persevere Saturday night, and then had a long ride home on Sunday.

As soon as I walked in, Bradford Hastings's secretary hallooed across the newsroom, "Al, Mr. Hastings has been waiting for you." When I entered his office, Hastings was studying notes he had taken on a yellow legal pad. The *Wall Street Journal* sat unopened on one corner of his large desk, a sign that the situation was serious.

"Sit down, Al," he said. He smiled perfunctorily. "The governor called this morning, Al. He's very upset, and I'm not sure I fully understand the situation."

"Mm."

"Can you explain what happened, Al?"

"No."

Hastings frowned and looked back down at his notes. "The governor says that you called on some banker . . . ," he scanned down the notes on the legal pad, "a Mr. Crew."

"Crowe, Rulon Crowe."

"And the governor says you told Mr. Crew that the state bank examiners are all controlled by environmentalists, and Mr. Crew is upset and so's the governor."

"Mm."

"Is that true?"

"No."

"Now, Al, would you give me an explanation, please."

"The story's in today's paper."

"Oh?"

"Yeah, it's small and runs inside. It's just about how the governor sent Mr. Crowe a letter commending him for his role in the CalCom deal. Why don't you have them run you in a copy? It's slugged 'banker.'"

Hastings was already punching a button on his phone. "Barry. Barry, could you run me in a copy of 'banker,' please?" Hastings frowned at his notes again.

"Now, Al, did you tell Mr. Crew that the bank examiners are controlled by environmentalists?"

"No, I didn't."

"What did you tell him?"

"I told him I had heard that bank examiners were coming to look at his books."

"The governor says that's totally false."

"Oh?"

"He said he had his staff call Financial Institutions this morning to check, and it is entirely without foundation."

"I told Crowe I might be wrong." A copy kid brought a printout of my story about Rulon Crowe and the governor's letter. Hastings read it quickly. It was only four paragraphs.

He said, "This doesn't have anything to do with bank examiners. What's going on here, Al?"

I paused to consider and then said, "I've figured out why Orson Jones was killed." That was the wrong thing to say. Hastings looked at once confused and slightly alarmed. He didn't understand what Jones had to do with our conversation, and in fact he needed a moment to remember who Jones was.

"Oh, the young man they found up by U Mountain, the one who worked for the government, isn't he?" Hastings finally said.

"Yes."

"Well, you should go to the police, and we ought to get the story first, then." Hastings forced a brief smile to reward his employee for a job potentially well done.

"Yes."

"But now back to this other matter, what should I tell the governor about why you told this Mr. Crew that the bank examiners were coming to his bank when they weren't?"

"Tell him I was misinformed. The story in the paper is accurate. There's no harm done."

"I'm afraid that won't do, Al." Hastings looked down at his legal pad and read from his notes. He marked the passage he wanted with his forefinger. "The governor said, and this is a direct quote, Al, a direct quote: 'Bank examiners act in strictest confidence, and for anyone to pretend to have inside information about their confidential activities is a slur on the integrity of my administration.'" Hastings looked up at me "That's what he said, Al, 'a slur upon the integrity of the administration.'"

Hastings sat back in his high-backed, black-leather, swivel chair and regarded me sternly. "Did some environmentalist tell you the bank examiners were going to Mr. Crew's bank?" he asked.

"No."

"Well, the governor says that somebody just fabricated the whole story. And he seems to think environmentalists are behind it. Is that right?"

"No."

"Where did you get this story about bank examiners, Al?"

"I made it up." Hastings's mouth opened and his eyes darted about in wild surmise. "I made up a story—most of it was true, but I made up the part about the bank examiners—to provoke Crowe and others into revealing what they are hiding about CalCom and Jones. I think it's going to work," I said.

Hastings was not reassured. "Al, we've got the governor more upset than I've ever seen him before, and you just made it up?"

"Yes."

"Why, Al? Why did you put the *Telegram* in this embarrassing position?"

"I told you, I've figured out why Jones was killed."

"Al, this isn't some crime story. This is the biggest opportunity for economic development Utah has ever had. This is about the future of our state and our community. We've explained to you that this is a sensitive story. We put you back on this story over Barry's objections because you're a seasoned member of the *Telegram* team, and we thought you understood the sensitivities." Hastings touched his fingers to his forehead as if he had a headache.

I spoke calmly. "I'll explain how it worked."

Hastings kept his head down and the fingers of one hand to his forehead. He made a pushing gesture with his other hand. He didn't want an explanation. After I thought a moment, I saw he was right. If I explained to him, he wouldn't understand and it would only make things worse. We sat quietly for a moment.

"I'm going to take you off this story, Al. You've lost your objectivity. I'll tell Barry to put another reporter on CalCom." He lowered his hand from his forehead. "And I want your promise, Al. I know how you maneuver in the newsroom and everything. I don't want you to have anything more to do with this story. I want that promise."

I pondered a moment. "No, I don't think so," I said.

Hastings's head jerked backward slightly. "What?" he asked.

"I've got a story here. I'm going to stay with it."

"Now, Al, there's no room for big egos at the *Telegram*. We all have to be team players."

"I think I'll stay with this."

Hastings looked at me hard. "I don't think that's what you want, Al. You've been at the *Telegram*, what? Twenty-four years?"

"Twenty-six. Only real job I've ever had."

Hastings leaned back in his seat and squinted at me. "Why are you doing this?"

I had to think why I was doing it. "All the years I've been here at the *Telegram* I've been on a leash. Sometimes I could find something out, sometimes I could get it in the paper. But if the governor or the Chamber of Commerce or the church knew about it, they could call up and the *Telegram* would pull my leash. That's what's happening now."

I had to think why I was doing it. "Maybe I've got the best story I ever had here. Up to now, you've pulled me off stories that upset things. I always wanted a story so good that I couldn't be pulled off. This may be the only chance I ever get."

"I can understand your frustration, Al. We all get frustrated sometimes. But we've got to live in this community. You understand that, Al. You're a pro."

"Yeah, I understand it," I said. "But I don't think I want to do it this time."

Hastings turned up his palms to show he was willing to be

reasonable. "Listen, Al, if you have a good story, just write it up. I'll look at it, and we can talk it over then. We always want to publish good stories."

I shook my head. "I'm not ready yet. I need to check things out. Do some more interviews."

"What you're saying, Al, is you don't really have the story yet. You've got rumors and speculation is all. Isn't that right?"

I nodded, "That's right."

"And these rumors and speculations probably come from environmentalists, don't they?"

"No, I thought them up myself."

"Well, Al, we can't have you running loose causing this kind of trouble and damaging the integrity of the *Telegram* just on wild speculation. You understand that." I nodded. We sat in silence for a while. He asked, "What are you going to do? Suppose you get the story, where are you going to publish it?"

"I don't know. I'll have to work something out."

"What are you going to do when this thing's over? Where will you work?"

"I don't know."

"You're a good reporter, Al, but you're getting older, and we can tell you, frankly, that among news executives you have a reputation for being difficult. It isn't going to be easy for you to get another journalism job."

"That's probably right."

"What else would you do, Al?"

"I don't know."

"You're not worried about it?"

"I'm terrified," I said. "If I don't have a job, I'll walk into a bar and never come out."

Hastings nodded. "To be perfectly honest with you, Al, that seems to us to be a very real worry. We hope you don't do that. We really hope you don't." Hastings looked down at his desk. "You know, we remember when we first came to the *Telegram*. What, you were in your third or fourth year here, something like that." Hastings looked up at the ceiling to calculate. "Yes, that would be right. You were the best reporter on any newspaper around here. No, really, you were. You had energy, you could write better than anyone else. Even then, you could understand what was going on. We thought pretty soon you'd leave and go to the *New York Times*, something like that."

"Didn't work out that way."

Hastings slapped the arms of his chair with both hands. "Al, we don't want this to happen. You've done things to make us proud here at the *Telegram*. We don't want to see you end up on the street."

"If I had a few more days to look around on the CalCom story, I think maybe I could wrap it up."

"I don't think we can give you that, Al." I nodded. "Listen, though," Hastings said. "We'll tell Barry to give you an interesting assignment, and after a while the governor will get over this. Then we'll see about getting you back on this CalCom story."

"I think I better do it now while it's still there."

"Are you going to leave then?" he asked.

"Yeah."

"Well, good luck to you." We shook hands, and I walked out of Hastings's office.

There wasn't much to clean out of my desk. I'd just moved back in and hadn't had time to re-accumulate the usual amount of junk.

I thought of saying good-bye to people in the newsroom, but decided maybe I'd do that later. I carried my stuff to my car, and then wondered what to do next.

I sat in the driver's seat of the car, looking at the cement interior of the parking terrace, and mused how I had given up my religion, my marriage, and now my career. Things were not going according to plan.

I looked at my watch. It was almost 11:00. I decided to go to D.B.'s, have a drink, early lunch, think things over.

thirty-one

The phone rang while I was still asleep. For a moment I thought the *Telegram* was calling and I had forgotten an assignment. I groped towards the ringing, trying to remember what I had missed so I could dictate a story. As I answered, I remembered I didn't have *Telegram* assignments anymore, and I wondered who else would call so early in the morning. "Al, this is Edith."

It was the *Telegram* after all. Now that I thought about it, I wasn't surprised. Bradford Hastings had obviously realized his mistake and wanted a reconciliation. He had his secretary call for an appointment so he could save face and avoid acknowledging his blunder directly. I could picture the meeting. Hastings would offer a "compromise" as a transparent cover for what would really be his surrender.

I would be gracious. I would not remind him how, in a foolish moment, he had risked losing the dean of the *Telegram* staff and damaging the institution he directed. But I must be firm. I would insist on a free hand on the CalCom story before I agreed to return. And come to think of it, I should certainly require a raise, too.

Edith said, "The governor's office called this morning. Janet Lundmon, do you know her?"

"Yes."

"I told her you don't work here anymore, but she wanted to talk to you anyway." Edith's tone implied she could not think why anyone would want to talk to me, now I that no longer worked at the *Telegram*.

"She wanted your home number, and I told her we don't give those. So she asked if I would call you as a favor and ask you to call her. She says it's urgent. The number's 538-1000."

"Yeah. Thanks."

Edith hung up and I went to the bathroom for some aspirin. I was disappointed that Hastings had not yet realized his error of yesterday, and I was annoyed, too. Now that I was no longer in the news business, the governor's office and the *Telegram* had no claim on my attention, especially not at a quarter to nine in the morning. If the *Telegram* wasn't calling to apologize, I really had nothing to discuss with them.

I dialed the governor's office. I had to wait on hold for a couple of minutes for Janet Lundmon. Then she said "Yeah, Al, thanks for calling. Did you leave the *Telegram*?"

"Yes."

"Why, what happened?"

"We had a disagreement over what I could report and publish in the paper."

"Oh? Is that all?"

"Yes."

"Well, I'm sorry. Do you know what you're going to do now?"

"No."

"You know, the news business is really getting mean these days. It doesn't matter how long you've been with them or anything. If you aren't making money for them, they just give you the axe."

I was about to interject and correct her misimpression, but she continued. "Listen, the gov's asked you to come to a meeting today, 11:00 a.m.. He wants to stop these rumors about CalCom and the Jones thing."

"He wants to talk to me about it?"

"Not just you. He's gonna get everyone involved together. I know this's short notice, but Rulon Crowe and Mayor Hafen are in town today, and so's this guy from Price, Pete Vassos. Do you know him?"

"Yeah."

"So the gov says this may be the only day he can get everyone together, and he asked me to make sure you were there."

"Okay."

"Good. You had me a little worried. I thought I could call you at work. Then they tell me you're not there anymore, and they won't give me your home number, and I was afraid you'd left town or something. The governor wants you there specifically. You'll come now?"

"Janet, I wouldn't miss it." I saw now what must be done, and the prospect of effective action was tonic. My head no longer ached, a general fuzziness had disappeared from the world.

I walked briskly toward the shower, then, on second thought, did an about face back to the phone. I wanted to make calls while I could catch people at their desks at the start of the day. I needed to talk to a man named Sullivan. My nephew Aaron would know his number. At family dinner with Uncle Moroni last Sunday, Aaron had said Sully was working on a real estate deal with Orson Jones,

maybe selling his house. I could see now how that was the key to
the whole puzzle.

thirty-two

When Governor Wells entered his office, all of us stood. He didn't shake hands as he normally would because there were so many of us. Instead, he faced us and nodded his head one-eighth of an inch in a little bow. Then he settled his bulk into the custom-made chair behind his desk, and we took our seats in three rows facing him.

"Thank you all for coming," the governor said. "I invited you here because I am concerned that certain interests may be using the tragic death of Orson Jones to spread rumors and innuendo which could be harmful to Utah's economic development." The governor's voice was grave, and his red face serious. His wavy, silver hair was perfectly in place and I imagined a trace of his cologne wafting in the office air.

Behind the governor's chair stood a credenza of dark oak with a copper plaque of the Great Seal of the State of Utah hanging in the center above his head and the Utah Code Annotated in twenty-eight blue, leather-bound volumes on the shelves. On the floor to the governor's right was a large globe, and next to it a shiny bronze elephant with his trunk upraised as if to trumpet Republicanism over all the earth.

Governor Wells sat up straighter to speak over our heads to Barbara Jones, who was sitting in the back. "Let me say at the outset, Mrs. Jones, you have our deepest sympathies on the tragic loss in your family." Then he added in sterner tones, "But we can't allow unsupported and perhaps malicious allegations to threaten Utah's economic development."

Mrs. Jones nodded. "I understand," she said. "I want to hear the discussion." All of the guests had been assigned seats by press secretary Janet Lundmon. On the first row from the governor's left to right were BLM chief Merrill Gott, my former boss Bradford Hastings, CalCom project chief Coleman Bywater, banker Rulon Crowe, and Mayor LaVar Hafen. Behind them in the second row were speculator Nick Vassos, speculator Bart Westerman, public relations man John Kilee, myself, and environmentalist Paul Rambeau. Barbara Jones, Lieutenant Wilford Banton, and Janet Lundmon sat in the rear.

The seating plan seemed clear to me. The important people would sit in the front row and talk. The less important people would sit in the second row and listen.

"Of course, my administration doesn't interfere in police business," Wells said. "Before I called this meeting, I spoke with Lieutenant Benton, who graciously agreed to be here. He assures me that we can have a frank and full discussion here today without compromising his investigation in any way. Do I understand that correctly, Lieutenant?"

"Yes, sir." Benton wore a blue tie and blazer, which I guess he wears only to go to court and on special occasions such as a meeting with the governor. Anyway, I'd never seen him in a coat and tie before.

"Now," the governor said, "I think the most pro-active strategy is to get everyone together and get all these allegations out on the table where everyone can see them and see if they hold up." He focussed on Coleman Bywater sitting in the middle of the front row. "Let me begin by asking you for the record, Coleman, did California Commonwealth have anything to do with the death of Orson Jones?"

"No sir, we did not."

"Thank you, Coleman. I wanted that stated formally by the leader of the CalCom Project so everyone could hear. I think one of the most damaging and malicious rumors has been that somehow CalCom is connected to this tragic—"

"With all due respect, this seems to be just part of the coverup," Rambeau interrupted from the end of the second row. He spoke in a matter-of-fact tone, but he tilted his head back, so his spade-shaped beard pointed combatively at the governor. "I think CalCom may have been involved, and this isn't just something that can be cleared up by a perfunctory denial at a meeting."

"Do you have any evidence, Mr. Rambeau?" the governor asked.

"I'm not an investigative agency," Rambeau said. "It's not my job to gather evidence. But it's clear CalCom benefitted from Orson Jones's death, and that fact requires careful investigation."

"Benefitted how?" Coleman Bywater asked. He turned and put his elbow on the back of his red-leather chair and looked intently at Rambeau through his dark-rimmed glasses. "I've never been able to understand how you say we benefitted."

"Well, for example, when Orson Jones was alive, you couldn't get your hands on the public's coal," Rambeau said evenly. "Just as soon as he's murdered, you get the coal, and this $10 billion juggernaut rolls forward again."

Public relations man John Kilee blurted at Rambeau, "No, you don't understand. We obtained another coal supply from Bart Westerman, here. We don't need the original coal. Orson Jones's death didn't help our project at all." When he finished speaking, he looked at Bywater for approval.

"That's right," Westerman said. "I got them all the coal they needed t'get this thing up and running." He sounded proud of his achievement.

"And for the record, another point," Merrill Gott said. He turned in his front-row chair to face Rambeau and paused with his mouth partly open and his thin upper lip curving upwards then down to a point in the middle. "Orson Jones's death didn't affect any decision we made at the Bureau of Land Management. Those decisions are reached in accordance with federal land management rules. Personnel considerations just aren't part of the equation."

Rambeau ran his eyes down the front row and saw five politely hostile faces. The governor's guest list assured the environmental point of view would not dominate the discussion. Though outnumbered, Rambeau was undaunted. He sharpened his attack. "I think what we're seeing here is an establishment that wants the CalCom Project so badly it's unified in blocking any investigation that might uncover unpleasant facts," he said.

Wells said promptly, "Lieutenant Benton, have I or any member of my administration interfered with your investigation in any way?"

"No, sir."

"Has anyone interfered in your investigation?"

"No, sir."

"Now see," the governor turned up both palms and ran his eyes over his assembled guests appealing to their candid judgment. "Here's another false rumor that could have damaged what we're trying to accomplish here. As the lieutenant just said, no one's blocking any investigation. We can see here again how my administration's pro-active strategy can help Utah."

I spoke. "I believe there is evidence that CalCom was involved in Orson Jones's death," I said.

"Oh?" the governor said. He raised his chin slightly and narrowed his eyes at me. He hadn't expected this.

"Orson Jones was murdered because of a conspiracy," I said. "And the conspirators are here in this room now."

thirty-three

Police Quiz Men in CalCom Case

For a moment the room was silent. Then Bradford Hastings said, "Just for the record, Al has left the *Telegram*, and we can take no responsibility for anything he says." I ignored Hastings because I had a long and complicated story to tell and didn't want to be diverted by minor matters.

"It began as a simple insider scam," I said. "A man who knew where the CalCom plant would be located before the location was publicly announced used that information to make an illegal profit." I looked to my right at Nick Vassos and Bart Westerman. "Specifically," I said, "he bought coal rights from Nick Vassos."

Vassos and Westerman both leaned forward to look at me. "Vassos spent fifteen years acquiring coal rights near Persevere in hopes of eventually selling to someone like Cal-

Com," I said. "He knew he took the risk that no one would want the coal and it would become worthless in the end. But the man with the scheme knew for certain that CalCom would pay a high price. So he bought the coal rights cheap, and with the prospect a sure thing."

Westerman said, "That's a lie." He looked at me belligerently from beneath his shiny, brown pompadour as if I had challenged him to a fight and he wasn't backing down.

"No, it's true," I said, keeping my voice mild. "In fact, you were the front man in the deal. The man—I'll call him Mr. X—couldn't buy the coal rights in his own name, so he got you to buy them for him. He told you where CalCom would locate and what to do, and you bought an option on Vassos's coal. Then after CalCom announced it would go to Persevere, you exercised the option, sold the coal to CalCom, and shared an enormous profit."

"You're lying," Westerman said, and he pointed his finger at me accusingly. But his effect was spoiled when he looked down and saw his finger was trembling. He put his hand back in his lap.

Coleman Bywater had turned around in his red leather chair and was looking from Westerman to me. "Look at the facts," I said to him. "Westerman had never made a coal deal before. He never even went to Persevere to look at this coal formation. Yet he knew exactly the right coal to buy at exactly the right time. The only way he could have known was that someone gave him inside information."

Bywater looked sternly at Westerman. Vassos glared at him, too. "I always thought you cheated me, but I didn't have no proof," Vassos said. He folded his beefy arms and looked away from Westerman in anger and disgust.

I got on with the story. "Vassos demanded cash, so Westerman and Mr. X needed money. They took a banker into the scheme to loan them the financing." On the front row, Rulon Crowe sat rigid and erect. He didn't turn to look at me. "Rulon Crowe loaned Bart

Westerman the money he needed to buy the coal leases," I said. "It wasn't a sound loan. The only collateral—"

The governor interrupted, "Al, you've been saying a lot of things lately about Rulon's bank that aren't true."

"What I'm saying now is true. Rulon Crowe's bank hasn't survived for three generations by making foolish loans. But this loan was for buying options on government coal. Speculating in coal is a standing joke in Persevere, and Crowe would never have made the loan if someone hadn't told him CalCom was coming." Crowe stared ahead as if he wasn't listening. "Probably he got a special payment or shares in Westerman's coal company, too," I said.

The governor said, "Al, you're just being plain irresponsible. Here you are attacking Rulon's character, and you were just let go at the *Telegram* for telling untruths about state bank examiners."

"I did go to Mr. Crowe last Saturday," I conceded. "And I told him that bank examiners would look into the loan he made on coal rights. I admit what I told him was false."

"Yes, it was," the governor interjected.

"I said it because I knew it would raise an alarm among the conspirators and force them to act." I looked at the governor and asked, "And that's exactly why you called this meeting, isn't it governor?"

Governor Wells's large, fleshy face turned a deeper shade of red. "No, Al, as I said already, I called this meeting to expose rumors that could damage Utah's economic development." He pointed a finger in my general direction. "But I'm glad at least we finally got the truth about the bank examiners."

I didn't want to argue with the governor. "If I could get back to the details," I said. "The scheme worked exactly as planned until the time came to sell the coal to CalCom and reap the profit. Then things began to go wrong. And that's what led to the murder of Orson Jones." For the first time, Crowe turned in his seat and stared at me in nearsighted surprise. Mayor Hafen was frowning at Crowe, as if he were weighing what I had said about the banker.

I said, "The first unforeseen problem arose when a consumer group got an order from the California Public Utilities Commission saying CalCom should not buy any more coal than necessary for the project. A woman named Virginia McCambridge called the *Telegram* about it." I turned to Bywater for confirmation. "You remember that, don't you, Mr. Bywater?"

"Yes, I do," Bywater said, nodding his head. "We had to make some adjustments in response to it."

"Specifically, CalCom decided to buy only Vassos's coal and not both Vassos's and Westerman's coal as originally planned," I said. "That way CalCom complied with the order from the California Public Utilities Commission."

"Yes, that's right," Bywater said. Public relations man John Kilee, who was sitting beside me, nodded his head in agreement with his boss.

"For CalCom, that was only an adjustment," I said. "But for the conspirators it threatened disaster. They had borrowed money to buy coal, and they suddenly had no place to sell it. Their option on the coal rights would soon run out. They faced ruin from an unexpected stroke of bad luck."

Kilee goggled at me through his thick glasses. I think he remembered the night at the Wasatch Front Club when Westerman boasted to him and me about confronting his banker when his loan was overdue and his options on coal rights appeared worthless.

"But though things looked bad, Mr. X was resourceful," I said. "He not only found a way to overcome his troubles, he actually used them to increase his profits. To do that he recruited Orson Jones into the conspiracy."

"No, sir. No," the governor interrupted, shaking his head and holding up both hands in a gesture to stop further talk. "Al, I won't have the deceased slandered in this office. What you're saying about Bart and Rulon here is bad enough. But at least they can defend themselves. Orson Jones can't. You're going too far." He stood up behind his desk. "I think we should end this meeting now."

"I have important information, Governor, and I think you should hear me out."

"No, I called this meeting to get rid of rumors, not to start new ones. This meeting is adjourned." Bywater stood up, and Kilee and Hastings followed him to their feet, ready to leave and break up the meeting.

"I don't believe this," Rambeau said loudly. "As soon as the facts about CalCom start coming to light, the power structure covers them up. I want you to know, Governor, I've been taking notes, and I'm certainly going to see that *60 Minutes* hears about what's gone on in this room." Wells glanced at Rambeau, and then started to walk out of the room.

"Governor, please," Mrs. Jones spoke from the back of the room. "I would like to hear what Mr. Cannon has to say."

Wells stopped, turned. He frowned while he thought of what to say to Orson Jones's widow. "Well, you can talk to Al privately then."

"It would help if we were all here," I said.

"We've heard enough already," the governor said and turned to resume his march to the door.

"Sir," Lieutenant Wilford Benton spoke softly. "I think it might help the investigation to hear this out." The governor gawked at the lieutenant.

"Please, governor," Mrs. Jones said. Governor Wells looked at Mrs. Jones, and then looked around the room, unsure of what to do.

"I'd like to hear what Al has to say," Hafen said as if casting his vote. The governor walked back behind his desk, plopped down in his custom-made chair, and glared at me from beneath his shaggy, gray eyebrows. Bywater, then Kilee, and finally Hastings sat down following the governor.

I hurried on with my story. "Orson Jones wrote a letter saying the federal government might not allow CalCom to mine their coal. I wrote a story about it in the *Telegram*. Jones pretended to write out of concern for the environment and the law, but in fact he was bribed to write that letter by Mr. X, who promised him enough money to buy a ranch. That letter saved the conspirators. CalCom took it to the Public Utilities Commission as evidence that the federal government might not let them mine the coal they had bought from Vassos. So the Commission gave them permission to buy more coal. And CalCom bought Westerman's coal as they had originally planned."

"They paid a higher price, too," Vassos growled.

"Yes, a lot more than you got," I said. "CalCom believed it was in a bind and needed Westerman's coal. The bind, of course, was fabricated. By using Jones, Mr. X had saved his scheme and increased his profits."

Rambeau objected. "I think you're wrong there, Al. I knew Orson, and I think he was too honest to sell out to industry. And his letter was right. That plant shouldn't be built."

"My understanding is the letter was contrary to BLM policy," I replied, "and he didn't tell his superiors he was writing it. Is that right, Mr. Gott?"

"Yes," Gott said in his rumbly voice. "The letter was clearly contrary to policy, and it would never have gone out if I had known about it. I think Orson was wrong to send it, but I don't think he was corrupt. He was the one who told you about the letter."

"Yes, he did tell me," I said. "He told me because the conspirators needed a delay. Selling coal to CalCom was a long, bureaucratic process, and the conspirators needed time to complete it."

I turned to Gott, "You told me you would have overruled Jones's letter before CalCom had to buy the extra coal if it hadn't been for the story in the newspaper."

"Yes, we would have, too," Gott said. "The story in the press forced us to take the issue to Washington. Then various groups got involved and caused considerable delay."

"Jones leaked the news of his letter to Rambeau, knowing it would be more believable if the leak came to a reporter from Rambeau than from himself." Rambeau frowned and looked down so his beard touched his chest.

"Then when I heard about the letter from Rambeau and called Jones, he pretended to be reluctant to tell me about it. But in fact, he intended all along for the press to learn about the letter. He was using me to gain the time Mr. X needed to sell the coal. And I admit, I was entirely fooled."

Rambeau spoke quietly. "You say Jones used me and used you in some plan to bilk money from the project. But you haven't shown any proof, and I still think he was an honest guy."

I nodded to concede my proof so far was thin, then supplied some evidence: "Earlier today, I called a man named Sullivan. He sells real estate. He said Orson Jones was looking to buy a ranch in the Persevere area. Jones planned to spend a couple-of-hundred-thousand dollars, according to Mr. Sullivan."

"What's his name?" Benton asked. He had his notebook out. I told him Sullivan's name and phone number.

Then I turned around in my chair to talk to Barbara Jones. "When I came to interview you the day your husband died, you said 'I knew it wouldn't work.' What did you mean?"

"I don't know what I meant," she said. "I don't remember saying that. I was so upset."

"It's true you were upset. But I think you also knew your husband was in some kind of scheme, didn't you?"

"No, I didn't know any . . ." She trailed off in midsentence and sat still for several seconds. "I didn't really know for sure, and I didn't want to know. I knew he was thinking maybe he could buy a ranch, and when I asked him about money he said he could take care of it. He wouldn't tell me about it and seemed worried and ashamed."

"You didn't tell Lieutenant Benton," I said. "He sensed you were holding something back. He thought maybe Orson was having an affair."

She shook her head. "Orson wouldn't do that."

"Why didn't you tell the police everything?" I asked.

Jones shook her head. "It's so unfair," she said. "He was a good man. He was a good man all his life. Then he did one thing, and he got killed. And now that's what everyone will remember him for." She bowed her head and rummaged in her purse for a handkerchief. "I thought nothing I do will bring him back. But maybe he won't be remembered for just one mistake."

She dabbed at her face with her handkerchief. "I kept thinking maybe I was wrong. I didn't really know, and I didn't want it to be true. And the kids, you know, they're so little now, they won't even remember him, hardly. They'll just know what people say. And I didn't want them to hear just that one thing. He wasn't like that. Not really." Hafen stood up, picked up his chair, and carried it to the back of the room. He set it beside Barbara Jones, sat down, and took her hand in both of his.

"He just thought it would be better if our kids grew up down in Persevere where he grew up," she said. "I'm okay," she sniffled in her hanky. "Go on. Please."

I went on. "The conspiracy would have succeeded. Mr. X had raised money, bought coal rights, overcome the commission order, maneuvered for the time they needed, and he was on the verge of an enormous profit. But then Mr. X was struck by his worst problem: Orson Jones had an attack of conscience. He wanted to get out of the scheme. He may even have planned to tell his boss at the BLM."

I turned to face Hafen who was still sitting beside Jones. "He told you he repented, didn't he?" I asked. "You said so at the funeral."

"I mentioned something like that at the funeral." Irritation sounded in Hafen's voice. "He didn't say anything specific, and I told you already I don't think it's right for me to talk about it."

"Could you tell me one thing?" I asked. "Did he say he was going to talk to anyone?"

Hafen raised his eyebrows in surprise at my guess. "Why, yes, he said there was a man he had to talk to. I don't know what he meant."

"Did he say who it was?" Benton asked.

"He didn't say a name."

"He talked to Mr. X," I said. "And I think we can see now who Mr. X is. Mr. X had to be someone with full inside knowledge of CalCom's business, enough knowledge so he could use Orson Jones in Utah to manipulate the Public Utilities Commission in California. And he had to know what the governor's office and the BLM were doing. He had to be someone credible enough to persuade Rulon Crowe to risk his bank on a loan to Bart Westerman. Mr. X is Coleman Bywater," I said.

Bywater had turned around in his front row seat to look at me. He had seen where I was heading, but he remained calm. "You were just fired from your job, Al. Have you become unbalanced?"

"No, you did it," I said. "You were disappointed when CalCom failed to pick you as president. Your finances were strained because of your divorce. So you planned to use your position on the project to profit by inside dealing in coal. And when Orson Jones told you he had changed his mind and would ruin your scheme, you hid up the canyon where he went jogging and murdered him."

The governor interrupted. "You said you had evidence, Al. But all I'm hearing is speculation."

"Think about it, Governor. You said you didn't understand when Coleman Bywater confirmed my story about Jones's letter.

You said it threw your timing off. You were right. He did it exactly for the purpose of throwing your timing off. He did it so he and his confederates would have time to sell their coal to CalCom and make a big profit."

A confused look came over the governor's ruddy face. "Is that true, Coleman?"

"It's ridiculous. There's no truth to it at all," Bywater said calmly. But the governor's perplexity continued to show on his face.

I turned to Kilee. "You can see it, too," I said. "You remarked how hard Bywater fought to get CalCom to buy Westerman's coal. You can see now that he fought for Westerman's coal because he owned a stake in it." Kilee goggled at me through his thick glasses, fidgeted in his chair, and made a barely perceptible nod. He was careful to avoid looking at his client.

I pointed at Bywater. "And Nick Vassos remembers that when he was dickering with Westerman you told him the whole project would probably be cancelled. That encouraged him to sell his coal."

"Yeah, that's right," Vassos said, looking at Bywater. "You said you was giving me information in confidence. I might notta sold, you hadn't told me that."

"But I think we have proof of fraud right here," I said. "Mr. Crowe, I told you examiners were coming to your bank. That was false when I said it, but I think it's true now. The whole of your bank and Westerman's business will be scrutinized by investigators. I don't think you'll be able to hide any dealings from them."

Crowe turned in his seat and peered at me nearsightedly down his grand nose. "And you may not want to keep secrets," I said. "All you did was make a bank loan. I don't think you had anything to do with the murder. But you can see clearly now that the loan you made and the facts you know are part of a larger conspiracy that resulted in the murder of Orson Jones. Do you still want to keep the murderer's secrets."

"No," Crowe said, "I don't want any . . ."

"You should not talk until you consult an attorney," Bwyater said quickly before Crowe could answer.

"No, I don't need to talk to a lawyer," Crowe said to Bywater. "He's right," he said, gesturing at me. "All I did was make a bank loan. You never told me Orson was involved. And I won't be part of his murder. He was a fine young man." Crowe turned toward the back of the room where Hafen sat with Jones. "Honestly, I had no idea Orson was involved in this until right now when Cannon told us."

"Did Coleman Bywater tell you CalCom would come to Persevere?" I asked.

"Yes, he told me the project would come if I made the loan to Westerman." Crowe spoke to the governor. "We made the loan because he assured us it would bring economic development to our community. You were kind enough to mention in your letter, Governor, that our bank has a long tradition of taking risks to promote our regional economy."

"Is that true, Coleman?" the governor asked again. His ruddy face had turned pale, and his mouth stayed open after he asked the question.

"You should be warned," Benton said, looking at Bywater, "that anything you say may be used against you in court." Bywater opened his mouth to talk but then decided to take Benton's warning and remained silent.

I spoke quickly to finish what I had to say. "I admit the murder will be harder to prove," I said. "One thing you should check, Lieutenant. You made a list of cars seen in the area the morning Jones was killed. You should check that list for a red Cherokee with California plates. That's a CalCom vehicle, and Bywater may have used it and then shipped it away so his own car wouldn't be recognized."

"Are you done?" Benton asked me.

"Yes, I'm finished."

"Mr. Bywater, Mr. Westerman, Mr. Crowe, would you come to my office, please? We need to talk about this," Benton said.

Bywater reached into his breast pocket and pulled out a black, leather day-planner. "I'm tied up right now, Lieutenant," he said. "I could meet with you later."

"No, sir, I'm afraid we can't wait," Benton said. "It'll have to be right now." As Benton spoke, I slipped out of the governor's office. If I hurried, I could still get the story in today's paper.

thirty-four

Myron Holmes Dies at Age 89

Coleman Bywater pleaded guilty to one count of second-degree murder. The prosecutor dropped capital murder, fraud, and bribery charges in return for the plea. "They call that prosecutor Monty Hall," Lieutenant Benton said.

"Monty Hall?" I asked.

"Yeah, *Let's Make a Deal*," Benton said. He didn't smile. "That's off the record," he said. Then a faint smile emerged. "I don't have to tell you it's off the record anymore, do I?" he said. "You aren't doing real news these days." Benton seemed pleased by my current difficulties at the *Telegram*, undeserved though they are.

Benton became serious. "What it was was capital homicide," he said. "It was a premeditated murder-type situation, and it was committed in furtherance of another felony, the fraud.

That's capital homicide. Maybe he shoulda dealt down to murder without the death penalty. But second degree?" Benton shook his big head. "Monty gave away too much."

"You couldn't prove capital homicide?"

"It was close," Benton said and nodded grudgingly that the evidence wasn't clear.

"You had Westerman and Crowe," I said.

He nodded. "They both made deals and agreed to testify. Westerman pleaded out to one count of fraud. I'd guess maybe eighteen months, two years. They just got Crowe on a misdemeanor. He won't do time."

"So you could prove the fraud."

"Fraud was no problem. Murder was hard."

Benton pressed his lips together. "Trouble was, Bywater never told Crowe or Westerman that he even brought Jones in on the deal, or at least that's what they say."

"You had Bywater at the scene," I said.

Benton pursed his lips and nodded. "Pretty good," he said. "We had a witness who saw the red Cherokee parked up by the gully. Saw it the day before, too. Bywater went up at least once before the crime, scouted the situation out, made sure that's where Jones ran. We can prove Bywater had the Cherokee at that time. But we can't prove for sure it was Bywater's Cherokee. The witness didn't remember the plate number."

"Did you ever find a cushion?" I asked.

Benton shook his head. "We thought maybe he sat up there on one of those cushions you take to football games to keep your bum warm, but if he did we never found it."

"You had the payment to Jones," I said.

Benton nodded. "I thought that repentance business was far-fetched. But as it turns out, that's the way it looks." Benton leaned back in his swivel chair until his head touched the gray metal file cabinet behind his desk. "Just before he wrote that letter about the coal, Jones opened an account at the Bank of Persevere for $40,000 cash. He deposits cash. Then just before he gets shot he closes the account. All the money out in a cashier's check. And Bywater deposits the cashier's check in an account he has in California.

"Looks like Bywater paid Jones in cash. Jones opened up an account, then decided he wanted out of the deal and he pays Bywater back with a cashier's check. Bywater waits up the canyon for him and blows him away. That's sure what it looks like."

"What does Bywater say?" I asked.

"Nothing."

"What'll he do?" I asked.

"Seven years." Benton shrugged, "I don't know. He's a smart guy. He'll tell the board this is his first offense. He's a clean, one-owner cream puff. He may be able to talk them into letting him out early."

"Seven years, then he'll be sixty-three, sixty-four. He'll be broke. It'll be hard," I said.

"Not hard enough," Benton said.

Mayor LaVar Hafen wasn't happy with the plea bargain, either. He came to the *Telegram* to see me when he was in Salt Lake on city business. "I read in the paper where Orson gave the money back before Bywater shot him," he said.

"Yeah."

"I'm glad he did that. He was a good man. Just went off the rails for a while is all."

"Yeah."

"It helps me anyway to know that," Hafen said.

"Is the project dead?" I asked.

"Officially, it's on hold," he said. He switched his Stetson from one hand to the other and crossed his legs as if he were putting things behind him and taking a position towards the future. "They say they'll come back and take a look at it when they get things sorted out. But I think it's dead, at least as far as Persevere's concerned."

"Rambeau's happy," I said.

The mayor shrugged. "Yeah, I don't know if we'd ever gotten it, anyway, with those environmentalists so opposed to it and everything."

"People upset?"

"We been disappointed before. We hoped for the project, of course. But we can keep going. Something else may come along."

"I hear Rulon Crowe won't be going to jail," I said.

"Yeah, I guess anymore that's his only good thing," the mayor said. "He's going to lose the bank. He's still feeling pretty shame-faced around town. First, he and his wife were going to move. Then once people understood he didn't have anything to do with killing Orson they were nice to him. Said he only made the loan to get the project, and everything. So Rule thought maybe he'd stay. Only now he's got to sell the bank. Regulators are pushing him. So maybe he's going to move after all." The mayor pressed his lips together in a grim expression as he thought of Crowe. Then his face softened. "I saw Barbara Jones," he said.

"How is she?"

"She's okay," he said. "Visiting her folks in Manti. I stopped and saw her on the way up this trip. She says she's just staying till she can get her feet back under her. Then she's going to come back up to Salt Lake and look for work. She's got a degree from the BYU, you know. I think she's going to be okay. Of course, it's always going to be hard on her and the kids," the mayor said. He stared at nothing in the middle distance and was quiet for a few seconds, then he looked at me. "It's awful hard on them." His face was solemn and his eyes were sad.

Barry Bowen wasn't happy, either. He stood by my desk holding an open copy of the *Deseret News* in both hands. The bottom of the paper rested against the porch of his fat stomach. "This is the worst I've ever seen," he said. "We had an exclusive on this Coleman Bywater story. Hastings jerks you off it and puts you on obits, and we're just getting killed. Look at this," he said rattling the *Deseret News.* "We needed you on this story, Al. You understand it."

"Hastings says I'm not a team player," I said. I was typing an obit into my word processor.

"Yeah," Bowen said. He read the *Deseret News* some more and then threw it into the newspaper recycling can with a flourish of disgust. "Look," Bowen said. "Maybe I could spring you for a couple of hours, and you could get us something on this Bywater thing. I mean it's your story, and we're just getting killed on it."

I shook my head. "I got work here, Barry. I really don't have time to do cop stuff if I do obits."

"Yeah," Bowen said. He kept his face neutral. We understood each other. I needed Bowen to go to Hastings and say he needed me back on news. If I gave Bowen stories, Hastings would trash them and keep me on obits just to make me miserable.

"It could have been a lot worse for me, Barry," I said. "I quit, remember. Hastings said he'd take me back, but I'd have to start here until he could see I would be a team player. I don't know if it would be smart for me to sneak off and do a story he doesn't want."

"Look, I'll talk to him," Bowen said. "I'll tell him we need you on this story. I mean you cracked the case. You came here and gave us an exclusive when you weren't even working here. I'll tell him we need you."

"If Hastings says it's okay, I think I can get you a good story on the Bywater case. I'd like to help you out."

Bowen walked towards Hastings's office. I went back to typing the obit. I doubt Barry can talk Hastings into anything now. He's still pretty mad. But eventually, of course, Hastings will see he needs the dean of Utah journalism back covering the news. He'll realize that any petty embarrassments with the governor should not be allowed to affect the way he runs the newspaper.

I'm not worried. I've seen trouble like this before.